Alessandro Baricco

AN ILIAD

Alessandro Baricco was born in Turin in 1958.
The author of four previous novels, he has won
the Prix Médicis Étranger in France and the
Selezione Campiello, Viareggio, and Palazzo al
Bosco prizes in Italy. He lives in Rome.

INTERNATIONAL

AN ILIAD

AN ILIAD

ALESSANDRO BARICCO

Translated from the Italian by Ann Goldstein

Vintage International
Vintage Books
A Division of Random House, Inc.
New York

FIRST VINTAGE INTERNATIONAL EDITION, AUGUST 2007

Translation copyright © 2006 by Alessandro Baricco

All rights reserved. Published in the United States by Vintage Books, a division of
Random House, Inc., New York. Originally published in Italy as *Omero, Iliade*
by Feltrinelli, Milan, in 2004. Copyright © 2004 by Giangiacomo Feltrinelli
Editore, Milano. This translation originally published in hardcover
in the United States by Alfred A. Knopf, a division of
Random House, Inc., New York, in 2006.

Vintage is a registered trademark and Vintage International and colophon are
trademarks of Random House, Inc.

The Library of Congress has cataloged the Knopf edition as follows:
Baricco, Alessandro, [date]
[Omero, Iliade. English]
An Iliad / Alessandro Baricco : translated from the Italian by Ann Goldstein.
p. cm.
1. Homer. Iliad. II. Goldstein, Ann, 1949–. III. Title.
PQ4862. A6745O4413 2006
853'.914—dc22
2005044681

Vintage ISBN: 978-0-307-27539-4

Book design by Soonyoung Kwon

www.vintagebooks.com

Printed in the United States of America
10 9 8 7 6 5 4 3

CONTENTS

A NOTE ON THE TEXT

A few lines to explain the origin of this text. Some time ago I had the idea of reading the entire *Iliad* in public, to evoke the story as it was originally disseminated in the Homeric world. When I found someone willing to produce such an undertaking (the Romaeuropa Festival, later joined by Torino Settembre Musica and Musica per Roma), it was immediately clear to me that in fact the text as it has come down to us was unreadable, at least as I was imagining: it would take some forty hours and an extremely patient audience. So I thought of intervening, to adapt it to a public reading. I had to choose a translation, and was guided by that of Maria Grazia Ciani, because it was in prose, and because, stylistically, it was close to my own feeling. And then I carried out a series of interventions.

First of all, I made some cuts to suit the patience of a modern audience. I almost never cut entire scenes, but confined myself, as far as possible, to removing repetitions, which in the *Iliad* are of course numerous, and concentrating the text a little.

I tried never to summarize but, rather, to create episodes that were more succinct while still made of portions of the original text. Thus the bricks are Homeric but the mortar and the resulting edifice are transformed.

I said that I almost never cut entire scenes. This is the rule, but there is one obvious exception: I removed all the appearances of the gods. As we all know, the gods intrude quite often in the *Iliad*, to direct events and sanction the outcome of the war. They are probably the aspect of the poem most extraneous to a modern sensibility, and often break up the narrative, diffusing a momentum that should rightly be palpable. I wouldn't have removed them if I had been convinced that they were necessary. But—from a storytelling point of view, and only that—they aren't. The *Iliad* has a strong structure of human agency that emerges as soon as the gods are sidelined. Behind every action of a god the Homeric text almost always cites a human one that duplicates the divine gesture and brings it, so to speak, down to earth. However much the divine exertions transmit a sense of the incommensurable so familiar in life, the *Iliad* shows a surprising obstinacy, still, in endowing events with a logic that has man as the ultimate actor. If, therefore, the gods are banished from the text, what remains is not so much a godless and inexplicable world as a very human story in which men live out their destiny as if fluent in a ciphered language whose code they know almost in its entirety. In sum: taking the gods out of the *Iliad* is probably not a useful way to gain an understanding of Homeric civilization, but it seems to me a very good way of bringing into relief the essentially human story obscured by the metaphysics of its age, retrieving the story and thus bringing it into the realm of contemporary narrative. As Lukács observed: the novel is the epic of a world deserted by the gods.

The second intervention I made is stylistic. Maria Grazia Ciani's translation is in a living language rather than a philological jargon. I tried to continue in that vein. From the lexical point of view I tried to eliminate the archaic that would distance us from the heart of things. And then I looked for a rhythm, a consistency of pace, the breath of a particular speed and a special slowness. I did this because I believe that to receive properly a text that comes from so far away in time it is necessary above all to sing it to our own music.

The third intervention is the most obvious, even if not as important as it might seem. I have made the narrative subjective. I chose several characters from the *Iliad* and let them tell the story, supplanting the external, unitary, Homeric narrator. For the most part, it's a purely technical move: instead of saying, "The father took his daughter in his arms," in my text the daughter says, "My father took me in his arms." It's obviously a stratagem dictated by the work's intended audience, just as Homer's method was suited to his. When Homer told his story the mythology and the characters were entirely familiar to his listeners. Today's audience would on the whole not know the particulars. At the same time, its expectations are for a certain intimacy that Homer cannot provide. At a public reading, giving the reader a modicum of personality to lean on, as it were, prevents him from slipping into a boring impersonality. And for the audience of today, hearing the story from those who lived it makes it easier to become involved.

Fourth intervention: naturally, I couldn't resist the temptation to make a few additions to the text. You will find them in italics, so that there is no equivocation: they are like forthright restorations, in steel and glass, on a Gothic façade. Quantitatively, these interventions make up a minimal percentage of the text. For the most part, they bring to the surface intimations that the *Iliad* could not express, given its own conventions, but hid between the lines. At times, they pick up pieces of the story handed down by other, later narrators (Apollodorus, Euripides, Philostratus). The most obvious case, although in a way anomalous, is the final monologue, that of Demodocus. As we know, the *Iliad* ends with the death of Hector and the return of his body to Priam: there is no trace of the horse and the fall of Troy. In the case of a public reading, however, it seemed to me treacherous not to tell how the war finally ended. So I borrowed a scene from the *Odyssey* (Book 8: at the court of the Phaeacians, an old bard, Demodocus, sings of the fall of Troy in the presence of Odysseus), and I set it inside, so to speak, the translation of some passages from *The Destruction of Troy,* by Triphiodorus, a book that probably dates from the fourth century A.D. and is not without a post-Homeric elegance.

The text that I thus obtained was read in public in Rome and Turin in the fall of 2004, and will probably continue to be read in the future, whenever some courageous producer finds the money to do it. For the record, I'd like to say that more than ten thousand (paying) people were present at the two readings, and that Italian radio broadcast the Rome performance live, to the great satisfaction of drivers on the road and people at home. Numerous cases were confirmed of people who sat in their parked cars for hours, unwilling to turn off the radio. All right, perhaps they were sick of their families, but, anyway, this is just to say that it went very well.

Now the text of this transformed *Iliad* is about to be translated into various languages, around the world. I realize that this adds paradox to paradox. A Greek text translated into an Italian text, which is adapted into another Italian text and finally translated into a text in, for example, Chinese.

Borges would undoubtedly have been ecstatic. The peril of losing the power of the Homeric original is certainly great. I can't imagine what will happen. But I'd like to warmly thank the publishers and translators who have undertaken to be my traveling companions on one of the most bizarre literary adventures ever contrived.

To the gratitude I feel toward them I'd like to add a homage to three people who helped me immensely during the gestation of this text. I would probably still be thinking about whether to do the *Iliad* or *Moby-Dick* if Monique Veaute hadn't decided, with her matchless optimism, that *first* I should do the *Iliad* and then *Moby-Dick*. What I now know about the *Iliad*, and didn't know before, I owe entirely to Maria Grazia Ciani: she followed this strange project with a kindness that I could never have expected. If, finally, the project became a book, I owe it yet again to the care of Paola Lagossi, my teacher and friend.

A.B., MARCH 2005

AN ILIAD

CHRYSEIS

It all began on a day of violence.

For nine years the Achaeans had besieged Troy: often they needed provisions or animals or women, and then they abandoned the siege and went to get what they wanted by plundering the nearby cities. That day it was the turn of Thebes, my city. They seized what they wanted and brought it to their ships.

I was among the women they carried off. I was a beauty: when, in their camp, the Achaean chieftains divided up the spoils, Agamemnon saw me and wanted me for himself. He was the king of kings, and the commander of all the Achaeans: he brought me to his tent, and to his bed. He had a wife, at home, called Clytemnestra. He loved her. But that day he saw me and wanted me for himself.

Some days afterward my father came to the camp. His name was Chryses, and he was a priest of Apollo. He was an old man. He brought splendid gifts and asked the Achaeans, in exchange, to set me free. As I said: he was an old man and a priest of Apollo. All the Achaean chiefs, after seeing and listening to him, were in favor of accepting the ransom and honoring the noble figure who had come to them as a suppliant. Only one among them was not won over: Agamemnon. He rose and railed brutally against my father, saying to him, "Go away, old man, and don't show yourself again. I will not give up your daughter: she will grow old in Argos, in my house, far from her homeland, working at the loom and sharing my bed. Go now, if you want to go with your life."

My father, frightened, obeyed. He went away in silence and disappeared along the shore of the sea—you might have said *into* the sound of the sea. Then, suddenly, death and suffering fell upon the Achaeans. For nine days, arrows flew, killing men and beasts, and the pyres of the dead blazed without respite. On the tenth day, Achilles summoned the army to a meeting. In front of all the men he said, "If things continue like this, we'll have to launch our ships and go home in order to escape death. But let's consult a prophet, or a seer, or a priest who can tell us what is happening and free us from this scourge."

Then Calchas rose, the most famous among the seers. He knew all the things that have been, are, and will be. He was a wise man. He said, "You want to know the reason for this, Achilles, and I will tell you. But swear that you will protect me, because what I'm going to say will offend a man who has power over all the Achaeans and whom all the Achaeans obey. I'm risking my life: swear that you will protect me."

Achilles told him not to be afraid, but to say what he knew. He said, "As long as I live, no one among the Achaeans will dare raise a hand against you. No one. Not even Agamemnon."

Then the seer took courage and said, "When we offended that old man, suffering came upon us. Agamemnon refused the ransom and would not give up the daughter of Chryses: and suffering came upon us. There is only one way to rid ourselves of it: restore to Chryses that girl with the sparkling eyes, before it's too late." Thus he spoke, and he sat down.

Agamemnon rose, his heart brimming with black fury and his eyes flashing fire. He looked at Calchas with hatred and said, "Prophet of doom, you have never given me a favorable prophecy. You like to reveal only evil, never good. And now you want to deprive me of Chryseis, whom I desire more than my own wife, Clytemnestra, and who rivals her in beauty, intelligence, and nobility of spirit. Must I give her up? I will do so, because I want the army to be saved. I will do it, if so it must be. But find me a prize to replace her immediately, because it is not right that I alone, among the Achaeans, should remain without honor. I want another prize for myself."

Then Achilles said, "How can we find you a prize, Agamemnon? The spoils have already been divided, and it wouldn't be fitting to start over again from the beginning. Give back the girl and we'll repay you three, four times over when we capture Ilium."

Agamemnon shook his head. "You don't deceive me, Achilles. You want to keep your prize and leave me with nothing. No, I will give back that girl and then I'll come and take what I like, and maybe I'll take something from Ajax, or Odysseus, or maybe I'll take something from you."

Achilles looked at him with hatred. "You insolent, greedy man," he said. "And you expect the Achaeans to follow you into battle? I didn't come here to fight the Trojans—they haven't done anything to me. They haven't stolen oxen or horses from me, or destroyed my harvest: my land is divided from theirs by shadowy mountains and a roaring sea. I'm here because I followed you, arrogant man, to defend Menelaus's honor and yours. And you, you bastard, dog face, you couldn't care less, and threaten to take away the prize I fought for? No, it's better that I return home rather than stay to be dishonored, fighting to win treasures and riches for you."

Then Agamemnon answered, "Go if you want, I won't beg you to stay. Others will gain honor at my side. I don't like you, Achilles: you love quarrel, strife, war. You're strong, it's true, but that's a gift. Leave, go home and rule in your own house. You are nothing to me, and I'm not afraid of your anger. Let me tell you this: I will send Chryseis back to her father, on my ship, with my men. But then I'll come to your tent and take for myself the beautiful Briseis, your prize, so that you'll know who is the stronger, and all men will learn to fear me."

Thus he spoke. And it was as if he had struck Achilles a blow to the heart. And the son of Peleus was about to unsheathe his sword and certainly would have killed Agamemnon if at the last minute he had not mastered his fury and stopped his hand on the silver hilt. He looked at Agamemnon and in a rage said:

"You with the face of a dog, the heart of a deer—you coward. I swear on this scepter that the day will come when the Achaeans, all of them, will long for me. When they are dropping under Hector's assaults, they will long for me. And you will suffer for them, but will be able to do nothing. You will only remember the day you insulted the best of the Achaeans, and go mad with rage and remorse. That day will come, Agamemnon. I swear it."

Thus he spoke, and hurled the gold-studded scepter to the ground.

When the assembly broke up, Agamemnon ordered one of his ships brought down to the sea, assigned to it twenty men, and put in charge Odysseus, the wily one. Then he came to me, took me by the hand, and led me to the ship. "Beautiful Chryseis," he said. And he let me return to my father and my homeland. He stood there, on the shore, watching the ship set sail.

When he saw it disappear over the horizon he called two men among his loyal followers and ordered them to go to the tent of Achilles, to take Briseis by the hand and lead her away. He said to them, "If Achilles refuses to give her up, then tell him that I will come and get her, and it will be much worse for him." The two soldiers were called Talthybios and Eurybates. They set off reluctantly along the shore of the sea and finally reached the camp of the Myrmidons. They found Achilles sitting beside his tent and his black ship. They stood before him and said nothing, because they were frightened and in awe of the king. So it was he who spoke.

"Come," he said. "You're not at fault in all this—Agamemnon is. Don't be afraid." Then he called Patroclus and told him to fetch Briseis and hand her over to the two soldiers, so that they could lead her away. "You are my witnesses," he said, looking at them. "Agamemnon is foolish. He doesn't think about what will happen, he doesn't think about when he might need me to defend the Achaeans and their ships. To him nothing matters in the past or the future. You are my witnesses, that man is a fool."

The men set off, retracing their path beside the swift ships of the Achaeans, drawn up on the beach. Behind them walked beautiful Briseis. Sadly she went—and reluctant.

Achilles watched them go. And then he went and sat alone on the shore of the white-foaming sea, and burst into tears, with the infinite ocean before him. He was the lord of the war and the terror of every Trojan. But he burst into tears and like a child began calling his mother. From far away she came, then, and appeared to him. She sat beside him and stroked him gently. Softly, she called him by name. "My son, why did I bring you into the world, I, your unhappy mother? Your life will be short enough. If only you could spend it without tears and without sorrow."

Achilles asked, "Can you save me, Mother? Can you do it?"

But his mother said only, "Listen to me: stay here, near the ships, and don't go into battle. Hold on to your anger against the Achaeans and don't yield to your desire for war. I tell you: one day they will offer you shining gifts, and they'll give you three times as many, for the insult you received." Then she disappeared, and Achilles sat there, alone. His soul was filled with rage for the injustice he had suffered, and his heart was consumed by yearning for the cry of battle and the tumult of war.

I saw my city again when the ship, commanded by Odysseus, entered the harbor. The sails were lowered, the ship approached the mooring under oars. The crew threw the anchors over and tied the stern ropes. First they unloaded the animals for sacrifice to Apollo. Then Odysseus took me by the hand and led me to land. He guided me to the altar of Apollo, where my father was waiting for me. He let me go, and my father took me in his arms, overcome with joy.

Odysseus and his men spent the night beside their ship. At dawn they raised the sails to the wind and departed. I saw the ship speed lightly as the waves foamed around the prow. I saw it disappear over the horizon. *Can you imagine what my life was then? Every so often I dream of dust, weapons, riches, and young heroes. It is always the same place, on the shore of the sea. There is the smell of blood and of men. I live there, and the king of kings throws to the winds his life and his people, for me: for my beauty and my charms. When I wake there is my father at my side. He caresses me and says, It's over, my daughter. It's all over.*

THERSITES

They all knew me. I was the ugliest man who went to the siege of Troy: bowlegged, lame, shoulders humped and curving in over my chest; a pointed head covered by a scraggly fuzz. I was famous because I liked to insult the kings, all the kings: the Achaeans listened to me and laughed. And so the kings of the Achaeans hated me. *I want to tell you what I know, so that you, too, will understand what I understood: war is an obsession of old men, who send the young to fight.*

Agamemnon was in his tent and he was sleeping. Suddenly he seemed to hear the voice of Nestor, who was the oldest of us all, our most beloved and respected sage. The voice said, "Agamemnon, son of Atreus, here you are sleeping, you who command an entire army and should have so many things to do." Agamemnon didn't open his eyes. He thought he was dreaming. Then the voice drew closer and said, "Listen to me, I have a message for you from Zeus, who is watching you from far away, and feels sorrow and pity for you. He orders you to arm the Achaeans at once, because today you will be able to take Troy by force. The gods, all of them, will be on your side, and your enemies will be doomed. Don't forget this when sweet sleep abandons you, and you wake. Don't forget this message from Zeus."

Then the voice vanished. Agamemnon opened his eyes. *He didn't see the old man Nestor, who slipped silently out of the tent.* He thought he had been dreaming, and that in his dream he had seen himself the victor. Then he rose and put on a new tunic, beautiful and soft, and over it a sweeping cloak. He put on his best sandals, and over his shoulder slung the silver-studded sword. Finally he seized the scepter of his fathers and, holding it tight in his fist, set out for the ships of the Achaeans, while Aurora announced the light of day to Zeus and all the immortals. He ordered the heralds, with their clear voices, to call the Achaeans to an assembly, and when they had all gathered he summoned first the noble princes of the council. He told them his dream. Then he said, "Today we'll arm the Achaeans and attack. But first I want to test the army, as is my right. I'll tell the soldiers that I have decided to give up the war and return home. You will try to persuade them to stay and continue the fight. I want to see what happens."

The noble princes were silent, uncertain what to think. Then Nestor the old man rose, Nestor himself, and he said, "Friends, leaders and rulers of the Achaeans, if any one of us should recount such a dream, we wouldn't listen to that man, thinking that he was lying. But he who dreamed it claims to be the best among the Achaeans. Therefore I say: let us go and arm our men." Then he rose and left the council. The others saw him going, and, as if following their shepherd, they all rose, in turn, and went to assemble their men.

As dense swarms of bees emerge from the hollow of a rock

and cluster over the spring flowers and disperse, flying from place to place, so the ranks of men came out of their tents and ships and lined up along the shore for the assembly. The earth rumbled under their feet, and everywhere chaos reigned. Nine heralds, shouting, tried to subdue the clamor so that all might hear the voice of the kings who were to speak. In the end they managed to make us sit, and the tumult ceased.

Then Agamemnon rose. He held in his hand the scepter that Hephaestus had made long ago. Hephaestus had given it to Zeus, the son of Cronus, and Zeus gave it to Hermes, the swift messenger. Hermes gave it to Pelops, tamer of horses, and Pelops to Atreus, shepherd of peoples. Atreus, dying, left it to Thyestes, rich in flocks, and from Thyestes Agamemnon received it, so that he might rule over all Argos and the many islands. It was the scepter of his power. He held it tight and said, "Danaans, heroes, followers of Ares, cruel Zeus has condemned me to a brutal fate. First he promised, he vowed, that I would go home only after destroying Ilium with its beautiful walls, and now he wants me to return to Argos without glory, and having sent so many of my men to their death. What a disgrace: a vast, shining armada battles a paltry force, and yet the end is still not in sight. We are ten times as many as the Trojans. But they have brave allies, who have come from other cities, and this, finally, will keep me from taking Troy the magnificent. Nine years have passed. For nine years our wives and our children have been at home waiting for us. The wood of our ships has rotted, and all the ropes are frayed. Hear me: let us flee on our ships and return home. We are never going to take the city of Troy."

Thus he spoke, and his words struck us to the heart. The immense assembly was shaken like a sea in a hurricane, like a field of grain tossed by a stormy wind. And I saw the people charge toward the ships, shouting with joy and raising a huge cloud of dust. They spurred one another to seize the ships and haul them down to the divine sea. They cleaned the keel channels, and, as they pulled the blocks out from under the hulls, their cries of yearning rose to the sky.

Then I saw Odysseus. Wily Odysseus. He hadn't moved. He hadn't gone to the ships. Anguish consumed his heart. Suddenly he threw off his cloak and hurried toward Agamemnon. He tore the scepter from his hand and without a word headed for the ships. And to the princes of the council he called out, "Stop. Don't you remember what Agamemnon said to us? He is testing them, but afterward he will punish them. Stop, and they, seeing you, will stop!" And with the scepter he beat any soldier he encountered, saying, "Stay here, you fool! Don't run away, you coward and deserter. Look at your leaders and learn from them." In the end he managed to stop them. From the ships and the tents they turned back, like the sea when it roars up onto the shore and then recedes, making all Ocean echo.

It was then that I decided to have my say. There, in front of them all, that day, I spoke. "Hey you, Agamemnon, what more do you want? What are you complaining about? Your tent is full of bronze, and full of beautiful women, too: the ones *you* choose when *we* give them to you after stealing them from their homes. Maybe you want more gold, brought by the Trojan fathers to ransom their sons, whom *we* take prisoner on the battlefield? Or is it a new woman you want, a woman to take to your bed, all for yourself? No, it's not right for a king to lead the sons of the Danaans to disaster. My friends, don't be cowards. Let's go home and leave him here in Troy to enjoy his spoils, then he'll see if we were useful or not. He has dishonored Achilles, a warrior a thousand times as great as he.

He has taken away Achilles' share of the spoils and now keeps it for himself. As for anger—if Achilles were really burning with rage, you, Agamemnon, would not be here insulting us again."

The Achaeans stood and listened to me. Many of them were enraged with Agamemnon because of what had happened with Achilles. So they listened to me. Agamemnon said nothing. But Odysseus, well, he came over to me. "You speak eloquently," he said to me. "But you speak like an idiot. You are the lowest of the low, you know, Thersites? The lowest of all the soldiers who came to the walls of Troy. You enjoy insulting Agamemnon, the king of kings, only because you Achaean fighters have brought him so many prizes. But I tell you, and I swear to you, that if I catch you saying stupid things like this again, I will take hold of you and strip off your clothes—cloak, tunic, everything—and send you naked back to the ships, wailing from a beating you won't forget." And so speaking, he began to hit me on the shoulders and the back with the scepter. I cringed under the blows. The blood dripped thick on my cloak, and I howled in pain and humiliation. Frightened, I fell to the ground. I lay there, dazed, drying my tears, while all around they laughed at me.

Then Odysseus raised the scepter, turned toward Agamemnon, and in a loud voice, so that all could hear him, he said, "Son of Atreus, the Achaeans today wish to make you the most wretched among mortals. They promised to destroy Ilium the fair and now instead they are weeping like boys, like miserable widows, and they ask to return home. Certainly I can't blame them: we've been here for nine years, when a mere month's absence from our wives would make us long to return. And yet what dishonor it would be to abandon the battlefield when we have spent so much time and gained nothing.

Friends, we must be patient still. Do you remember the day we assembled in Aulis, ready to depart, on our way to destroy Priam and the Trojans? Do you remember what happened? We were offering sacrifices to the gods near a spring, under a lovely, light-dappled plane tree. And suddenly a serpent with a blood-red back, a horrible monster that Zeus himself had created, emerged from under the altars and slithered up the tree. There was a nest of swallows above, and he went up and devoured all of them: eight little ones and the mother. And immediately afterward he was turned to stone. We saw it all and were struck dumb. But Calchas—do you remember what Calchas said? 'It's a sign,' he said. 'Zeus has sent us a sign. It is an omen of infinite glory. Just as the serpent devoured eight little ones and the mother, so we will have to fight in Ilium for nine years. But in the tenth year we will take Troy and its broad streets.' This he said to us. And today you see that prophecy fulfilled before your eyes. Listen to me, Achaeans with your weapons of war. Do not run away. Stay here. And we will capture the great city of Priam."

Thus he spoke. The Achaeans gave a loud shout, and the ships resounded with the tremendous clamor of their enthusiasm. Just then, the old man Nestor spoke again, saying, "Agamemnon, return and lead us into battle with your old indomitable will. No one wants to hurry home before he's slept with the wife of a Trojan, to avenge what we've suffered for the abduction of Helen. And I tell you that if anyone, in his foolishness, decides to go, then he won't get as far as his black ship before he meets his destined death."

In silence they listened to him. Old men . . . Agamemnon almost bowed. "Yet again, old man, you've spoken wisely." Then he looked out over all of us and said, "Go and prepare, because today we will attack. Eat, sharpen your spears, get

your shields ready, feed the swift horses well, check your chariots: we'll fight all day, and only night will separate the fury of
men. Your chests will drip with sweat under the heavy shields,
and your hands will grow weary holding the spears. But anyone who dares to flee the battle and take shelter near the ships
is a dead man."

Then they all gave a huge cry and scattered among the
ships. Each went to prepare himself for battle. Some ate, some
sharpened their weapons, some prayed, some made sacrifices
to the gods, hoping to escape death. Soon the kings of divine
descent assembled the men and drew them up in their battle
lines, rushing among them and urging them on. And suddenly
for us all it became sweeter to fight than to return to our
homeland. We marched in our bronze armor, and we were like
a fire that you watch from a distance as it devours a forest: you
see the bright shining flames flaring into the sky. We descended
to the plain of Scamander like a huge flock of birds that
descends from the sky and lands on the meadow with a great
din, wings beating hard. The earth rumbled under the feet of
men and the hooves of horses. We stopped near the river,
before Troy. We were thousands, as many as the flowers in
spring, and we wished for one thing only: the blood of battle.

Hector and his allies, the foreign princes, assembled their men
and came out of the city, on foot or with horses. We heard an
immense commotion. We saw them ascending the hill of
Bateia, a hill that rose, isolated, in the middle of the plain.
There they ranged themselves, under the command of their
chiefs. They began to move toward us, shouting like birds in
the sky that with their screeching cries proclaim a mortal
struggle. And we marched toward them, but in silence, with
the anger hidden in our hearts. The footsteps of our armies

raised a dust that, like a fog, like a night, consumed everything.

Finally we came face-to-face. We stopped. And then, suddenly, from the ranks of the Trojans Paris stepped forth, like a god, a leopard skin flung over his shoulders. He was equipped with bow and sword. In one hand he held two bronze-tipped spears, and he shook them at us, challenging the Achaean chiefs. When Menelaus saw him, he rejoiced like a hungry lion who hurls himself on the body of a deer and devours it. He thought that the moment had come to take revenge on the man who had stolen his wife. And he leaped out of his chariot, grasping his weapons. Paris saw him and his heart trembled. He turned away, among his men, to avoid death. Like a man who sees a snake and immediately jumps back, shaking, and flees, his face pale, so we saw him run, until Hector stopped him, shouting, "Damn you, Paris, you seducer, liar. Don't you see that the Achaeans are mocking you? They thought you were a hero because they were impressed by your beauty. But now they know you have no courage and no strength of mind—you who, a guest of Menelaus, in a foreign land, carried off his wife and came home with that beautiful woman at your side. But they are a warrior people, Paris, and you have become the ruin of your father, of your city, of all your countrymen. And now you won't confront Menelaus? Too bad, you might find out what sort of man he is whose wife you stole. And you would roll in the dust, and discover how useless your lyre is, and your handsome face, and your hair. Ah, we are truly cowards, we Trojans: otherwise you would be buried under a pile of stones by now, to pay for all the evil you have done."

Then Paris answered, "You're right, Hector. But what a heart you have, inflexible, like an axe that plunges straight into the wood. You reproach me for my beauty . . . but we can't despise the gifts of the gods, the talents they've given us: can we refuse them? Do we have any choice in them? Listen to me: if you want me to fight a duel, have all the Trojans and all the Achaeans sit down, and let Menelaus and me, in front of the two armies, fight for Helen. The one who wins will take the woman and all her wealth. And as for you, Trojans and Achaeans, you will make a pact of peace, and the Trojans will live again in the fertile land of Troy, and the Achaeans will return to Argos, to their treasures and their beautiful women."

Hector's joy was great when he heard those words. He walked, alone, between the two armies and, raising his spear to the sky, made a sign to the Trojans to stop. And they obeyed. We immediately began to take aim at him with arrows and stones, and then Agamemnon cried, "Stop! Achaeans, do not strike him, Hector wants to speak!" and then we, too, stopped. There was a great silence. And in that silence Hector spoke to the two armies: "Listen to me! Hear what Paris says, the man who caused this war. He wants you to lay down your arms, and asks to fight alone against Menelaus, and let a duel decide who will have Helen and her wealth."

The armies remained silent. Then the powerful voice of Menelaus was heard. "Listen to me as well: I am the offended one and more than anyone else have a wrong to avenge. Stop fighting, because by now you have all suffered too much from this war that Paris started. I will fight him, and destiny will decide which of us two must die. You find a way to make peace as quickly as possible. Let the Achaeans go and offer a lamb to Zeus. And you, Trojans, get a white lamb and a black one, for the Earth and the Sun. And summon the great king Priam, so that he may sanction the peace: his sons are proud and not to be trusted, but he is an old man, and old men know how to look at the past and the future together, and understand what's best for all. Have him come and seal the peace: and may no one dare to break a pact sanctioned in the name of Zeus."

I heard his words and then I saw the joy of those two armies, suddenly united by the hope of putting an end to the agonies of war. I saw the warriors descend from their chariots and take off their arms and lay them on the ground, covering the plain with bronze. *I had never seen peace so close. Then I turned and looked for Nestor, the old sage Nestor. I wanted to look him in the eyes, and in his eyes see war die, and the arrogance of those who wish for it, and the folly of those who fight it.*

HELEN

Like a slave, I was silent in my rooms that day, forced to weave on a blood-colored cloth the exploits of the Trojans and the Achaeans in that grievous war fought for me. Suddenly Laodice, the most beautiful of Priam's daughters, entered and called to me, "Hurry, Helen, come and look down, Trojans and Achaeans . . . they were all on the plain, eager for blood and about to fight, and now they are silent, facing each other, with their shields resting on the ground and their spears planted in the earth . . . It's said that the war has stopped, and that Paris and Menelaus are going to fight for you: you'll be the winner's prize."

Suddenly, listening to her, I wanted to cry, because I felt a powerful yearning for the man I had married, and for my family, and my country. I wrapped myself in a shining white veil and ran to the wall, my eyes still filled with tears. When I reached the tower above the Scaean gates I saw the old men of Troy, who had gathered there to watch what was happening on the plain. They were too old to fight, but they liked to talk—and in that they were masters. Like cicadas in a tree, they never stopped to listen to their own voices. I heard them murmuring, when they saw me, "It's not surprising that Trojans and Achaeans should kill one another for that woman— doesn't she seem a goddess? But I wish the ships would take her away, her and her beauty, or our ruin and that of our children will never end." Thus they spoke, but without daring to look at me. The only one who looked was Priam. "Come, daughter," he said to me, raising his voice. "Come and sit beside me. You aren't to blame in all this. It's the gods who have brought this misfortune on me. Come, from here you can see your husband, and your relatives, your friends . . . Tell me, who is that imposing man, that noble Achaean warrior? Others are taller but I have never seen one so handsome, so stately: he has the look of a king."

Then I went to him and answered, "I honor and fear you, Priam, father of my new husband. Oh, if only I had had the courage to die rather than follow your son here, abandoning my marriage bed, and my daughter, still a child, and my beloved companions . . . but it was not so, and now I am worn out with weeping. But you want to know who that man is. He is the son of Atreus, Agamemnon, the most powerful king and a brave fighter: at one time, if that time ever existed, he was the brother-in-law of this worthless woman who is now talking to you."

Priam went on looking down at the fighters. "And that man," he asked, "who is he? Shorter than Agamemnon but his chest and shoulders are broader. Do you see him? He is reviewing the ranks, and is like a thick-fleeced ram wandering among flocks of white sheep."

"That is Odysseus," I answered, "the son of Laertes, who

grew up on the rocky island of Ithaca and is famous for his cunning and his intelligence."

"It's true," said Priam. "I've met him. He came here once as an envoy, with Menelaus, to discuss your fate. I welcomed them in my house. Menelaus, I recall, spoke quickly, a few clear words. He spoke well, but he was young . . . Odysseus, on the other hand . . . when it was his turn to speak, he didn't move. He looked down as if not knowing what to say: he seemed overcome by anger or else a complete fool. But when, finally, he spoke, a voice emerged so deep . . . the words were like winter snow . . . and no man would have dared challenge him, my daughter, and it didn't matter if he was shorter than Menelaus or Agamemnon . . ."

Then among the fighters Priam discerned Ajax, and asked me, "And that man, who is bigger and stronger than all the other Achaeans, who is he?" And I answered, and spoke to him of Ajax, and then of Idomeneus, and then of the other Achaean chiefs. I could recognize them all now, the bright-eyed Achaeans. One by one I could have talked of them to that old man, who wanted to know who his enemies were. But at that point Idaeus, the herald, arrived. He approached Priam and said, "Rise, son of Laomedon. The leaders of the Teucrians, breakers of horses, and of the bronze-armored Achaeans invite you to descend to the plain, to approve a new agreement between the two armies. Paris and Menelaus with their long spears will fight for Helen. All the others will seal a pact of friendship and peace."

Priam listened, and he shuddered. But then he ordered horses to be brought, and when everything was ready he got into his swift chariot, along with Antenor, and they went out of the Scaean gates at a gallop. They crossed the plain, and when they reached the armies they stopped right in the middle, between Trojans and Achaeans. I saw Agamemnon stand, and with him Odysseus. The heralds brought animals for the sacrifices that would seal the pacts. They mixed the wine in the great bowl, and poured water over the hands of the kings.

Then Agamemnon raised his hands to heaven and prayed to Zeus in the name of all. "Father Zeus, supreme and glorious, and you, Sun, who see all and hear all; Rivers, Earth, and you who under the earth punish traitors, be our witnesses and preserve our pacts: if Paris kills Menelaus, he will take Helen and all her possessions, and we will go away forever on our ships that plow the sea; and if Menelaus kills Paris, the Trojans will give us Helen and all her possessions, and will pay the Argives a price so high that it will be remembered for generations and generations. And if Priam and his sons are unwilling to pay, I will fight for that recompense, and remain here, until this war ends."

So he prayed, and then with a sure stroke he slaughtered the lambs and laid them, trembling as they died, on the ground. All the chiefs drank from the great wine bowl and prayed to the gods. And they said to one another, "If anyone dares to violate the pacts, may Zeus pour out his brains and those of his children as we pour this wine!" When everything was done, Priam, the old king, the old father, climbed into his chariot beside Antenor and said to the Trojans and the Achaeans, "Let me return to my wind-whipped city, because I don't have the heart to watch my son Paris fight here with fierce Menelaus." He spurred on the horses himself, and went off.

Then came the duel. Hector and Odysseus marked out on the ground the area where the two men would fight. Then they placed lots in a helmet, and, after shaking them, Odysseus, without looking, drew the name of the one who would be first to hurl the deadly spear. And fate chose Paris. The warriors were sitting all around. I watched Paris, my new husband, put on his armor: first the fine greaves, fastened with silver pins; then the breastplate over his chest; and the bronze sword studded with silver, and the big heavy shield. He placed on his head the shining helmet: the tall crest blew in the wind, stirring fear. Finally he grasped the spear and held it tight in his fist. Opposite him, Menelaus, my old husband, finished putting on his armor. Under the eyes of the two armies they advanced, looking at each other fiercely. Then they stopped, and the duel began. I saw Paris hurl his long spear. Violently it struck Menelaus's shield, but the bronze didn't crack, and the spear broke and fell to the ground. Then Menelaus in turn raised his spear and hurled it at Paris with enormous power. It hit in the middle of the shield and the deadly point tore through and pierced the breastplate, grazing Paris in the side. Menelaus drew his sword and rushed at him. He struck him hard on the helmet, but the sword broke. He cursed the gods and then with a leap grabbed Paris by the head, hands clutching the shining plumed helmet. And he began to drag him toward the Achaeans, Paris lying in the dust and he, holding the helmet in a murderous grip, dragging him, until the leather strap that held the helmet in place under his chin broke and Menelaus found himself with the helmet empty in his hands. He raised it to the sky, turned to the Achaeans, and, swinging it in the air, tossed it among them. When he turned again toward Paris, he saw that he had escaped, disappearing among the ranks of the Trojans.

It was at that moment that the woman touched my veil and spoke to me. She was an old seamstress who had come with me from Sparta, and had sewed splendid garments for me there. She loved me, and *I was afraid of her*. That day, up on the tower above the Scaean gates, she came to me and in a low voice said, "Come, Paris awaits you in his bed. He has put on his finest garments—as if he had returned from a feast rather than a fight."

I was astonished. "Miserable creature," I said to her, "why do you want to tempt me? You would be capable of bringing me to the ends of the earth if a man there was dear to you. Now, because Menelaus has defeated Paris and wants to take me home, you come to me plotting deception . . . You go to Paris. Why don't you marry him, or become his slave? I will not go, it would be dishonorable. All the women of Troy would feel shame for me. Let me stay here, with my grief."

Then the old woman looked at me in fury. "Be careful," she said, "and don't make me angry. I could abandon you here and sow hatred everywhere, until you would find yourself dying a miserable death." *She frightened me, I told you. Old people, often, inspire fear.* I held the shining white veil tight around my head and followed her. They were all looking down toward the plain. No one saw me. I went to Paris's rooms and found him there. A woman who loved him had enabled him to enter Troy through a secret gate and had saved him.

The old woman took a chair and placed it facing him. Then she told me to sit. I did. I couldn't look him in the eyes, but I said to him, "So you escaped the battle. I wish you were dead, killed by that magnificent warrior who was my first husband. You who boasted you were the stronger . . . You should go back and challenge him again. But you know very well that it would be the end of you."

I remember that then Paris asked me not to hurt him with my cruel insults. He said to me that Menelaus had won that day, because the gods were on his side, but maybe the next time he would win, because he, too, had friends among the gods. And then he said to me: Come, let's make love. He asked if I remembered the first time, on the island of Cranae, the day after he abducted me. And he said to me: Not even that day did I desire you as much as I desire you now. Then he rose and went to the bed. And I followed him.

He was the man who in that moment everyone down on the plain was searching for. He was the man whom no one, neither Achaean nor Trojan, would have helped or hidden that day. He was the man they all hated, as the black goddess of death is hated.

PANDARUS · AENEAS

My name is Pandarus. My city is Zelea. When I left to go and help defend Troy, my father, Lycaon, said to me, "Take horses and chariot to lead our people into battle." We had in our splendid palace eleven new, magnificent chariots, and for each chariot two horses fed on white barley and spelt. But I didn't take them. I didn't listen to my father and went to war alone, with bow and arrow. The chariots were too beautiful to end up in a battle, and the animals, I knew, would only suffer hunger and fatigue. So I didn't have the heart to take them with me. I left with bow and arrow. Now, if I could go back, I would break that bow with my hands and throw it in the fire to burn. In vain I brought it with me, and my fate was unhappy.

Paris had just vanished into nothing, and the armies stared at each other mutely, wondering what to do. Was the duel over? Had Menelaus won, or would Paris return to fight? Just then

Laodocus, the son of Antenor, approached and said to me, "Hey, Pandarus. Why don't you shoot one of your arrows and take Menelaus by surprise, now? He's standing there in the middle, defenseless. You could kill him, you've got the skill. You would be the hero of all the Trojans, and Paris, I'm sure, would cover you with gold. Think about it?"

I thought about it. *I imagined my arrow flying to its target. And I saw the war end. It's a question you could think about for a thousand years and you would never find an answer: Is it permissible to do a vile thing if by doing so you can stop a war? Is betrayal forgivable if you betray for a just cause? There, amid my people in arms, I didn't have time to think about it. Glory drew me, and the idea of changing history with a simple, precise action.* So I grasped my bow. It was made from the horns of an ibex, an animal that I had hunted myself: I had killed it with a shot under the breastbone as it was jumping down a cliff, and from its horns, sixteen palms long, I had had my bow made. I stood it on the ground and bent it to hook the string, made of ox sinew, to the gold ring fixed at one end. My companions, around me, must have understood what I had in mind, because they raised their shields to hide and protect me. I opened my quiver and took out a new, swift arrow. Briefly I addressed a prayer to Apollo, the god who protects us archers. Then I pinched together arrow and string and pulled them back until my right hand came to my chest and the point of the arrow was steady at the bow. With all my strength I bent the ibex horn and stretched the ox sinew until they formed a circle.

Then I shot.

The bowstring whistled and the sharp-pointed arrow flew swiftly, high above the men. It struck Menelaus just where the gold clasps fasten the breastplate to the war belt. The tip cut through the fastenings, through the leather band that protects the belly, and reached his flesh. Blood oozed along his thighs, down his legs, to his slender ankles. Menelaus shuddered when he saw the black blood, and so, too, did his brother Agamemnon, who immediately went to him. He took him by the hand and began to weep.

"My brother," he said, "have I perhaps sent you to die by making a foolish pact with the Trojans, under which you fought, alone and defenseless, before our eyes? Now the Trojans, who swore to the pact, have wounded you, breaking our agreement . . ." Agamemnon wept. He said, "If you die, Menelaus, I will die of grief. No Achaean will stay and fight here. We'll leave your wife, Helen, to Priam, and I'll be forced to return to Argos in disgrace. Your bones will rot here, beside the walls of Troy, and the proud Trojans will trample on them, saying, 'Where is Agamemnon, the great hero, who brought the Achaean army here only to return home with empty ships, leaving his brother on the battlefield?' Menelaus, don't die: if you die the earth will open up beneath me."

"Don't be afraid, Agamemnon," Menelaus said to him. "And don't frighten the Achaeans. You can see, the point of the arrow hasn't gone all the way into the flesh, it's just grazed it. First the breastplate and then the belt deflected it. It's a slight wound."

"If only that may be true," said Agamemnon. Then he ordered the heralds to call Machaon, the son of Asclepius, who was famous as a healer. They found him in the ranks of the army, among his men, and led him to where fair-haired Menelaus lay wounded. Around him were all the bravest Achaean warriors. Machaon leaned over Menelaus. He pulled the arrow from the flesh, observed the wound. Then he sucked the blood and skillfully applied soothing drugs that the centaur Cheiron had once given to his father in friendship.

They were still gathered around Menelaus when we Trojans began to advance. We had all taken up our arms, and in our hearts had only a desire for battle. Then we heard Agamemnon call to his men: "Argives, may you be strong and brave. Zeus does not help traitors, and those men whom you saw violate our agreement will be devoured by vultures, while we, having conquered their city, will carry off on our ships their wives and children." He was no longer the hesitant and doubtful Agamemnon we knew. That was a man who wanted the glory of battle.

We advanced in a tumult of sound. We were of different lands and peoples, and each cried out in his own tongue. We were a herd of beasts with a thousand different voices. The Achaeans, instead, marched in silence. You heard only the voices of the commanders giving orders, and it was something to see all the men obey, submissive, without a word. They came toward us like waves toward the rocky shore. Their armor sparkled like the foam of the sea spraying along the crest of the waves.

When the two armies met, there was a huge crashing of shields and spears and fury of armed men in bronze. The convex leather shields collided, and cries rose, of joy and grief intertwined, of the dead and the living, all mixed up in a single immense roar in the blood that soaked the earth.

AENEAS

The first to kill was Antilochus. He hurled his spear at Echepolus and struck him in the middle of the forehead: the bronze tip pierced the skull, under the crested helmet. Echepolus fell like a tower, in the midst of the brutal fight. Then Elephenor, leader of the bold Abantes, grabbed him by the feet and tried to drag him out of the fray in order to strip off his armor as quickly as possible. But to pull the body he had to leave his side unprotected, and just there, where his shield couldn't cover him, Agenor struck. The bronze spear penetrated the flesh and carried away his strength. Over his body a tremendous struggle was unleashed between Trojans and Achaeans; they were like wolves that attack each other and kill for the prey.

Then Telamonian Ajax struck Simoisius, the young son of Anthemion, struck him on the right side of the chest; the bronze spear passed through his shoulder, and the hero fell to the ground, in the dust, like a branch cut and left to dry beside a river. Ajax was stripping him of his armor when a son of Priam, Antiphus, saw him and from a distance hurled his spear. It missed Ajax but hit Leucus, one of the companions of Odysseus: he was hauling off a corpse when the bronze tip pierced his belly. He fell, dead, on the dead man he was pulling by the arms. Odysseus saw him fall and his heart swelled with anger. He went up to the front lines and looked around, as if seeking prey; the Trojans retreated before him. He raised his spear and hurled it, swift and powerful, through the air. It struck Democoon, a bastard son of Priam. The bronze point entered his temple and pierced the skull. Darkness descended over his eyes, and the hero fell to earth. His armor thundered down around him.

Then Pirous, the leader of the Thracians, attacked Diores, the son of Amarynceus. With a sharp rock he hit him in the right leg, near the heel: it broke the bone, severed the tendons. Diores fell to the ground. He felt that he was dying and reached out his arms to his companions. But Pirous arrived instead and with his spear ripped open his stomach: the guts poured out on the ground, and darkness covered his eyes.

And Thoas attacked Pirous, striking him in the chest with his spear, piercing his lung. Then he pulled out the spear, grasped the sharp sword, and tore open his stomach, taking his life away.

Slowly the battle began to turn in favor of the Achaeans. Their commanders, one by one, challenged ours, and each time won. First, Agamemnon, lord of peoples, knocked the great Odius, the commander of the Halizonians, out of his chariot. And as Odius tried to escape, Agamemnon struck him in the back with his spear, running him through. The hero fell with a great din, and his armor thundered down upon him.

Idomeneus killed Phaestus, the son of Borus of Maeonia, who had come from the fertile land of Tarne. He hit him in the right shoulder as he was trying to get out of his chariot. The hero fell backward, and darkness enveloped him.

Menelaus, the son of Atreus, struck Scamandrius, the son of Strophius. He was an extraordinary hunter: Artemis herself, it seemed, had taught him to kill the wild animals that live in the woods and the mountains. But that day no god helped him, nor did his death-bearing arrows save him. Menelaus of the glorious spear saw him running away, and the spear caught him between the shoulder blades and emerged from his chest. The hero fell forward, and his armor thundered down upon him.

Meriones killed Phereclus, who had built for Paris the well-made ships, the beginning of the disaster. His hands knew how to fashion any sort of beautiful object. But Meriones pursued him, hitting him in the right buttock, and the point of the spear went straight through, beneath the bone, and tore the bladder. The hero fell to his knees with a cry, and death enveloped him.

Meges killed Pedaeus, the bastard son of Antenor, whose wife nevertheless reared him as her own son, to please her husband. Meges struck him in the head, in the back of the neck. The spear passed through his skull and cut off his tongue. The hero fell in the dust, teeth biting the cold bronze.

Eurypylus killed Hypsenor, the priest of Scamander, who was venerated by all the people as a god; he pursued him as he tried to flee, and when he reached him drew his sword and sliced through one shoulder, cutting off the arm. The bloody arm fell on the ground, and over the eyes of the hero dark death and implacable fate descended.

PANDARUS

We fled and, fleeing, found death. The worst was when Diomedes, the son of Tydeus, appeared, right in the midst of the fray. Diomedes, the brave Achaean commander: the armor gleamed on his shoulders and his head, he sparkled like the autumn star as it rises from Ocean. He descended from his chariot and raged across the plain like a torrent in flood, swollen by rains. Nor could you tell if he was among the Achaeans or us Trojans: he was a river that had broken its banks and flowed swiftly onward, destroying everything in its path. It seemed nothing could stop him: I watched him fighting, and it was as if a god had decided to fight at his side.

Then I took my bow yet again. I stretched the ox sinew with all my strength and let the arrow fly. It struck him in the right shoulder, on the breastplate. The arrow pierced the flesh and went straight through to the other side. His breastplate was stained with blood. I shouted, "Attack, Trojans, Diomedes is wounded, I've hit him!" But I saw that he didn't fold, didn't fall. One of his companions pulled the arrow out of his shoulder: the blood spurted on the armor and all around. And then I saw him return to the fight, looking for me, like a lion who, though wounded, doesn't die but, rather, triples his fury. He attacked the Trojans as if we were a flock of terrorized sheep.

I saw him kill Astynous and Hypiron: the first he struck in the chest with his spear; with his sword he cut off the arm of the second. Nor did he stop to strip their armor but went after Abas and Polyidus. They were the two sons of Eurydamas, an old man who knew how to interpret dreams: but he was unable to read those of his sons, the day they left home, and Diomedes killed them both. I saw him attack Xanthus and Thoon, the only sons of old Phaenops: Diomedes took them from him, leaving him alone with his tears and his grief. I saw him slaughter Echemmon and Chromius, sons of Priam. He leaped into their chariot the way lions tackle bulls to break their necks, and killed them.

At that point Aeneas came looking for me. "Pandarus," he said, "where is your bow, and your winged arrows and your reputation? Did you see that man who is raging through the fighting, killing all our brave men? Maybe he's a god who's angry with us. Take an arrow and strike him as you alone can do."

"I don't know if he's a god," I answered. "But that crested helmet, and the shield, and those horses—I know them, they belong to the son of Tydeus, Diomedes. I shot an arrow at him and hit him in the shoulder, but he returned to the fight. I thought I had killed him, and instead . . . This damned bow of mine makes the blood of the Achaeans run but doesn't kill them. And I have no horses, no chariot, to ride into battle."

Then Aeneas said to me, "We'll fight together. Climb into my chariot, take the reins and the whip, and lead me to Diomedes. I'll get out of the chariot to fight him."

"You take the reins," I said. "If for some reason we're forced to flee, the horses will take us away more quickly if it's your voice that's guiding them. You drive the chariot and leave the fighting to me and my spear."

So we mounted the shining chariot and, full of fury, urged the swift horses toward Diomedes. They were the best horses ever seen under the light of the sun: they came from a race that Zeus himself had created as a gift for Tros. In battle they were terrifying. But Diomedes wasn't frightened. He saw us coming and he didn't run. When we reached him I shouted, "Diomedes, son of Tydeus, my swift arrow, my bitter dart, didn't bring you down. Now my spear will." And I threw it. I saw the bronze tip pierce the shield and strike his breastplate. Then I shouted again. "I've won, Diomedes, I got you in the stomach, stuck you straight through." But he, fearless, said, "You think you got me. But you missed the target. And now you won't leave here alive." He raised his spear and hurled it. The bronze tip entered near the eye, went through the white teeth, cut the tongue cleanly at the base, and came out the neck. I fell from the chariot—I, a hero—and the bright shining armor thundered down upon me. The last thing I recall is the swift, terrible horses as they swerved in panic. Then my strength abandoned me, and, with it, life.

AENEAS

The bronze tip entered near the eye, went through the white teeth, cut the tongue cleanly at the base, and came out the neck. Pandarus, the hero, fell, and the bright shining armor thundered down upon him. His strength abandoned him, and, with it, life. I knew that I had to get him away, that I couldn't let the Achaeans have his body and his armor. So I jumped down from the chariot and stood beside him, raising spear and shield, and shouting at all who approached. I found myself facing Diomedes. He did something incredible. He picked up a rock that two men, I swear, could never have lifted. And yet he did it, he lifted it up over his head and threw it at me. It struck me in the hip where it meets the thigh. The sharp stone ripped the skin and tore the tendons. I fell to my knees, placed one hand on the ground, felt a dark night descend over my eyes: *and I discovered suddenly what my destiny was: to never die.*

I heard Diomedes approaching, to kill me and strip me of my armor. Three times I heard him arrive, and yet I was still alive. Around me my companions fought, shouting, "Diomedes, what do you think you are, an immortal god?" I heard the voice of Acamas, the commander of the Thracians, calling, "Sons of Priam, don't you see that Aeneas needs you? How long will you let the Achaeans go on killing your men? Will you let them drive you back to the walls of the city?" And as someone pulled me back, I heard the voice of Sarpedon, prince of the Lycians, shouting, "Hector, where is your courage? You said that you would save your city without the help of allies, you alone, you and your brothers. But I don't see any of you here fighting. You're cowering somewhere, like dogs around a lion. And it's up to us, your allies, to lead the battle. Look at

me, I've come from far away, I have nothing here for the
Achaeans to plunder, and yet I urge my soldiers on to defend
Aeneas and battle Diomedes—while you, on the other hand,
aren't even moving, or commanding your men to resist. You'll
end up the prey of your enemies, you and your city."

When I opened my eyes again I saw Hector jump down
from his chariot, brandishing his weapons and calling his
men to battle. Sarpedon's words had stung his heart, and he re-
kindled the harsh fight. Finally the Trojans attacked. And the
Achaeans waited, white with the dust stirred up by the hooves
of their horses. Fearlessly they waited, as still as the clouds that
Zeus gathers above a mountain peak on a calm day.

I am Aeneas, and I cannot die. For that reason I was back in
the battle. Wounded but not dead. Saved by the fold of some
god's shining robe, hidden from my enemies, and then pushed,
again, into the heart of the battle, against Crethon and
Orsilochus, valiant warriors in the prime of life, who followed
the Achaeans on their black ships to honor Agamemnon and
Menelaus. I killed them with my spear, and they fell like tall fir
trees. Menelaus saw them fall and took pity on them. Clothed
in shining bronze he moved toward me, brandishing his spear.
Antilochus came, too, to help him. When I saw them, together,
I retreated. When they reached the bodies of Crethon and
Orsilochus, they picked them up and laid them in the arms of
their companions, and again rushed into the fray. I saw them
attack Pylaemenes: he fought from his chariot while his charioteer, Mydon, guided the horses. Menelaus ran him through
with his spear and killed him. Mydon tried to drive the chariot
away, but Antilochus hit him in the elbow with a rock, and the
white reins, adorned with ivory, slipped from his hands, into

the dust. Rushing at him with his sword, Antilochus stabbed him in the temple. Mydon staggered, the horses flung him out of the chariot.

Then came Hector, leading all the Trojans. The Achaeans saw him approaching and began to retreat, frightened. Hector killed Menesthes and Anchialus, but he couldn't carry off their bodies. And Ajax killed Amphius, but he couldn't get his armor. Sarpedon, lord of the Lycians, and noble Tlepolemus, the son of Herakles, faced each other. The spears left their hands at the same moment. Tlepolemus was hit in the neck: the bitter point passed through him, and dark night descended over the hero's eyes. Sarpedon was hit in one thigh, and the eager bronze penetrated to the bone. His companions seized him, without even pulling out the spear. The long spear was heavy, but they carried him off, like that. And Odysseus, seeing his companion Tlepolemus die, rushed to finish off Sarpedon. He killed Coeranus and Alastor and Chromius, and Alcander and Halius and Noëmon and Prytanis. He would have gone on killing if Hector hadn't suddenly appeared, clothed in shining bronze, terrifying.

"Hector," Sarpedon cried, lying wounded on the ground, "do not abandon me to the hands of the Achaeans. Save me. Let me die, if I must die, in your city." Hector said nothing; he went on driving his enemies away. Seeing him, the Achaeans began to retreat, not turning to flee but no longer fighting. And Hector, advancing, killed Teuthras and Orestes, and Trechus, and Oenomaus and Helenus and Oresbius. "Shame on you, Achaeans!" Diomedes cried. "When glorious Achilles was taking part in the war, then the Trojans were terrified, they didn't even dare to leave their city; now instead you let them get all the way to your ships!" Thus he cried. And the battle extended everywhere, throughout the plain: everywhere between the waters of Xanthus and those of Simois men were pointing their bronze spears at one another. Ajax was the first to rush forward and break the Trojan ranks. He struck Acamas, the most valiant among the peoples of Thrace. The point of the spear entered his forehead and penetrated the bone. Darkness descended over his eyes.

Diomedes, with a powerful cry, killed Axylus, the son of Teuthras, who was rich and beloved of men. He welcomed all to his house, which was right along the road, but no one, that day, came to defend him from bitter death. Diomedes took his life away and that of his driver: both descended underground.

Euryalus killed Aesepus and Pedasus, the twin sons of Bucolion. He cut off life and vigor from their handsome bodies; from their shoulders he took their weapons.

Polypoetes killed Astyalus, Odysseus killed Pidytes, Teucer killed Aretaon, Eurypylus killed Melanthius, Antilochus killed Ablerus. Agamemnon, lord of peoples, killed Elatus.

I saw all the Trojans running back, desperately, toward their city. I remember Adrastus, whose horses, mad with fear, stumbled on a tamarisk bush, throwing him to the ground; and immediately Menelaus was on him. Adrastus embraced his knees and begged him, "Don't kill me, Menelaus. My father will pay any ransom for my life, bronze, gold, well-wrought iron, whatever you want." Menelaus was persuaded and was about to leave him to one of his men to be led, a prisoner, to the ship when Agamemnon rushed over to him and cried, "Menelaus, you're a weakling. What do you care for these people? Don't you remember what the Trojans did in your house? None of them must escape our hands and the abyss of death, none, not even those who are still hidden in the bellies of their mothers. None must escape—let them all perish together with Troy, without a grave and without a name."

Adrastus was still kneeling on the ground, terrified. Menelaus pushed him away. And Agamemnon himself thrust the spear in his side and killed him. Then he placed his foot on his chest and ripped the spear point out of the flesh.

The Achaeans pressed and we fled, overcome by fear. We were at the walls of Troy when Helenus, one of Priam's sons, came toward me and Hector and said, "We must stop our men before they flee into the city and take refuge in the arms of their women, to the scorn of our enemies. Aeneas, we'll stay and fight and urge the men on, and you, Hector, meanwhile, go into the city and tell the people to pray to the gods to keep at least Diomedes away, who is fighting like a madman, and whom none of us can stop. We were never so afraid even of Achilles. Trust me, Hector. Go to our mother and tell her that if she has pity on Troy and on our wives and our children, she is to take the finest and largest robe in the palace and lay it on the knees of shining-eyed Athena, in the temple high in the citadel. We'll stay here, urging on the men and fighting."

Hector listened to him. He jumped down from his chariot and ran to the Scaean gates. I saw him disappear among the men: he ran, with his shield thrown behind his back, and the edges of the shield, of black ox hide, hitting his neck and heels. I turned. The Achaeans were before us. We all turned. As if a god had descended to fight at our side, we attacked.

THE NURSE

Of course I remember that day. I remember everything about that day. And that alone is what I want to remember. Hector arrived. He came through the Scaean gates and stood under the great oak. All the wives and children of the Trojans ran to him: they wanted news of their sons and brothers and husbands. But he said only: Pray to the gods, because disaster is hanging over us. Then he hurried to the palace of Priam. An immense palace, with shining porticoes. What splendor . . . on one side, fifty rooms of polished stone, built one beside the other: there slept the male children of Priam, with their wives. And on the other, twelve rooms of polished stone, built one beside the other: there slept the daughters of Priam with their husbands. Hector entered and Hecuba, his gentle mother, went to him. She took him by the hand and said, "My son, why are you here? Why have you left the battle? The hated Achaeans are crushing you there, against the walls. Have you come to lift up your arms to Zeus, from the height of the citadel? Let me give you some wine so that you may drink and offer it to the gods. Wine can revive a weary man, and you are exhausted, you who are fighting to defend all of us."

But Hector said no. He said that he didn't want wine, he didn't want to lose his strength and forget about the battle. He said to her that he couldn't offer wine to the gods, either, because his hands were stained with dust and blood. "Go to the temple of Athena," he said to her. "Take your finest robe, the largest one you have in the palace, the one you love most, and go and lay it on the knees of Athena, the predator goddess. Ask her to have pity on the Trojan wives and their little children, and pray to her to get rid of Diomedes, the son of Tydeus, because he is a savage fighter, and is sowing fear everywhere."

Then the mother called her handmaidens and sent them throughout the city to gather the old women of noble birth. Then she went into the scented chamber where she kept the robes embroidered by the women of Sidon, robes that godlike Paris had brought home from his journey when he returned with Helen, crossing the wide sea. And among all the robes Hecuba chose the finest and largest, embroidered all over, which shone like a star. And I want to tell you this: it was at the bottom, the one that was lying under all the others. She took it and set off with the other women to the temple of Athena.

In truth, I wasn't there. But I know these things because they were talked about, always, among us, the servant women, and all the palace attendants. And they told me that Hector, when he left his mother, went to look for Paris, to bring him back to the battle. He found him in his room, polishing his beautiful armor, the shield, the breastplate, the curved bow. Helen, too, was in the room. She sat among her women. They were all working with marvelous skill. Hector entered—still with the spear in his hand, the bronze tip gleaming—and as soon as he saw Paris he cried out, "You shameless man, what are you doing here, giving in to bitterness while men are fighting beneath the high walls of Troy? It's you who are the cause of this war. Come on, come and fight, or you'll soon see your city in flames."

Paris . . . "You are not wrong, Hector, to reproach me," he said. "But try to understand. I am here not to nurse resentment against the Trojans but to feel my sorrow. Helen, too, is telling me gently that I must return to the battle, and perhaps it's the best thing I can do. Wait for me, for the time it takes to put on my armor, or go on ahead and I will join you."

Hector didn't even answer. In the silence all the women heard the sweet voice of Helen. "Hector," she said, "how I wish that on the day my mother brought me into the world a stormy wind had carried me far away, to some mountain peak or into the waves of the sea, before all this happened, or that fate had, at least, kept for me a man who was able to feel shame and the scorn of others. But Paris doesn't have a strong nature, and never will. Come here, Hector, and sit beside me. Your heart is oppressed by troubles and it's my fault, the fault of me and Paris and our folly. Rest beside me. You know, sorrow is our fate: but for that reason our lives will be sung forever, by all the men who come after."

Hector didn't move. "Don't ask me to stay, Helen," he said. "Even if you do it for my sake, don't ask. Let me go home, rather, because I want to see my wife and my son: my family. The Trojans fighting out there are waiting for me, but still I want to go to my wife and son, see them, because I truly don't know if I will ever return here again, alive, before the Achaeans kill me."

Thus he spoke, and he went away. He came to his house

but he didn't find us. He asked the servants where we were and they told him that Andromache had gone to the walls of Ilium. She had heard that the Trojans were giving way before the power of the Achaeans and she had rushed to the walls, and the nurse with her, carrying little Astyanax in her arms. And now they were out there, rushing like madwomen toward the walls.

Hector didn't say a word. He turned and headed swiftly toward the Scaean gates, crossing the city again. He was about to leave and return to the battle when Andromache saw him and ran to stop him, and I behind her, with the small, tender child in my arms, the beloved son of Hector, bright as a star. Hector saw us, and he stopped. And smiled. *This I saw with my own eyes. I was there.* Hector smiled. And Andromache went up to him and took his hand. She wept and said, "Unhappy Hector, your strength will be your ruin. Don't you feel pity for your son, who is still a child, and for me, your unlucky wife? Do you want to go back there, where the Achaeans all together will attack you and kill you?" She wept. And then she said, "Hector, if I lose you, it will be better to die than to live, because there will be no comfort, for me, only sorrow. I have no father, no mother, I have no one anymore. Achilles killed my father when he destroyed Thebes with its tall gates. I had seven brothers and Achilles killed them all, on the same day, while the slow oxen and the white sheep grazed. Achilles carried off my mother, and we paid a ransom to get her back, and she returned to our house, but only to die, suddenly, of grief. Hector, you are my father, and mother, and brother, and you are my husband, and young. Have pity on me. Stay here, on the wall. Don't fight out in the open plain. Lead the army back to the wild fig tree, which marks the only weak point of the wall, where the bold Achaeans have already attacked three times."

But Hector answered, "I know all this, woman. But the shame I would feel if I were to stay away from the battle would be too great. I was taught, growing up, always to be strong, and to fight in the front line of every battle, for the glory of my father and for my own. How could my heart now allow me to flee? I well know that the day will come when the sacred city of Troy will perish, and with it Priam and the people of Priam. And if I imagine that day it's not the grief of the Trojans that I imagine, nor that of my father, or my mother, or my brothers, slaughtered by their enemies and lying in the dust. When I imagine that day I see you. I see an Achaean warrior who seizes you and drags you away in tears, I see you a slave, in Argos, weaving clothes for another woman and fetching water for her at the fountain, I see you weeping, and I hear the voices of those who, seeing you, say, 'Look there, that's the wife of Hector, the bravest of all the Trojans.' May I die before I know you are a slave. May I be under the earth before I have to hear your cries."

Thus spoke glorious Hector, and then he came toward me. I was holding his son in my arms, you see? And he approached and was going to take the boy. But the child hugged my breast and burst into tears. It frightened him seeing his father. The bronze armor frightened him, and the fluttering crest on the helmet scared him, and so he burst into tears. And I remember that then Hector and Andromache looked at each other and smiled. He took off the helmet and set it on the ground. Then the child let himself be held, and Hector took him in his arms and kissed him. And lifting him up high he said, "Zeus, and you other gods in heaven, let my son be like me, the bravest of all the Trojans, and lord of Ilium. And may people seeing him return from battle say, 'He is even braver than his father.' May he return one day bearing the bloody spoils of his enemies, and may his mother be there, that day, to rejoice in her heart." And as he was speaking these words he put the child in Andromache's arms. And I remember that she smiled and wept, hugging the child to her breast. She wept and smiled, and Hector, looking at her, took pity on her and caressed her and said to her, "Don't grieve too much in your heart. No one will kill me unless fate wills it; and if fate wills it, then remember that no man, once he is born, can escape fate. Whether he is a coward or brave. No one. Now go home and take up your work at the spindle and the loom with your women. Let the men take care of the war, all the men of Troy, and I more than any other man of Troy."

Then he bent down and picked up his helmet from the ground, the helmet with the fluttering crest. We went home. Andromache wept as she walked, and kept turning to look back. When the women saw her coming, a great sadness arose in all of them. They burst out crying. They wept for Hector. They wept for him in his house, wept for him while he was still living, because not one felt in her heart that he would return from the battle alive.

NESTOR

We saw Hector come hurrying out of the Scaean gates. We thought he had returned to fight, but in fact what he did was strange. He strode along the front ranks of his men, with his spear lowered, ordering them to stop. So Agamemnon, too, ordered us Achaeans to lower our arms. Thus the two armies faced each other, suddenly silent, almost motionless: they were like the sea when the wind begins to blow and the surface lightly ripples. In the middle of that sea was Hector, and he spoke out.

"Hear me, Trojans, and you, Achaeans. I will tell you what is in my heart. The gods delude us with their promises, and then condemn us to suffering and sorrow, and so it will go on until Troy wins or is taken. And so I say to you: if there is an Achaean prince who has the courage to fight me, man to man, I challenge him. Today I am ready to meet my fate."

The armies were silent. We, the Achaean princes, looked into one another's eyes: it was clear that we were afraid to accept the challenge, but we were ashamed to refuse it. Finally we heard the voice of Menelaus, furious.

"So, Achaeans, what are you, sissies? Can't you imagine the disgrace if no one of us accepts the challenge? Go to your ruin, men without courage or glory. I will fight for you, and the gods will decide the victor." And he took his armor and stepped forward. We knew that it was hopeless, that Hector was too strong for him. So we stopped him. Agamemnon, his brother, took him by the hand and spoke to him in a low voice, gently. "Menelaus, don't continue in this madness. Don't fight a man who is stronger than you. Even Achilles is afraid to fight Hector, and you want to do it? Stop, let us send someone else."

Menelaus knew in his heart that Agamemnon was right. He listened and obeyed: he let his men take the armor from his shoulders. Then I looked at all the others and said, "Alas, what a sad moment this is for the Achaean people. How many tears would our fathers shed if they knew that we were all trembling before Hector. Ah, if only I were still young and strong. I would not be afraid, I swear, and Hector would have to fight me. You are afraid, I wouldn't be."

Then nine of them stepped forward, first Agamemnon, and then Diomedes, the two Ajaxes, Idomeneus, Meriones, Eurypylus, Thoas, and, last, Odysseus. Now they all wanted to fight. "Fate will decide," I said. And in Agamemnon's helmet I had each of the nine put a tile bearing his symbol. I shook the helmet and drew one. I looked at the symbol. Then I went to Telamonian Ajax, the only one of us who had some hope against Hector, and gave it to him. He looked. He understood. And throwing it on the ground he said, "Friends, mine is the fate, mine is the fortune, and my heart laughs, because

I will crush glorious Hector. Give me my arms and pray for me."

He dressed in dazzling bronze, and when he was ready he went toward Hector with long strides, terrifying, brandishing his spear on high, above his head, with a fierce expression on his face. Seeing him, the Trojans trembled, all of them, and I know that even Hector felt his heart race in his chest. But he could no longer flee, having thrown out the challenge, and he couldn't withdraw.

"Hector," Ajax shouted, "now you'll find out what sort of heroes there are among the Achaeans, besides Achilles the destroyer. He, the lion-hearted, may be in his tent, but, as you see, we, too, are capable of fighting you."

"Stop talking," Hector answered, "and fight." He raised his spear and hurled it. The bronze tip struck Ajax's enormous shield, tore through the layer of bronze and then, one after the other, seven layers of ox hide, and in the last it stopped, in the last layer, just before it would have wounded him. Then it was Ajax's turn. The spear tore through Hector's shield. Hector leaned to one side, and this saved him. The bronze tip only grazed him. It tore his tunic but didn't wound. Then both wrenched the spears from the shields and set upon one another like savage lions. Ajax was protected by his enormous shield; Hector kept striking but couldn't touch him. When he grew tired, Ajax left the shelter of his shield and with a thrust of the spear cut his neck: we saw the black blood spurt from the wound. Another would have stopped, but not Hector: he bent down to pick up a stone from the ground, huge, jagged, black, and he hurled it at Ajax. You could hear the shield resound—the bronze echoing—but Ajax withstood the blow and in his turn picked up a rock, an even bigger one, swung it in the air, and threw it with a terrible strength. Hector's shield broke apart and he fell, but right away he got up again, and they grabbed their swords and went for one another, yelling . . .

And the sun set.

Then two heralds, one Achaean, one Trojan, came forward to separate the two, because even in battle it's good to be obedient to the night. Ajax didn't want to stop. "It's Hector who must decide, he made the challenge." And Hector decided. "Let's interrupt the fight for today," he said. "You are strong, Ajax, and your spear is the best among all those of the Achaeans. You will make your friends and companions happy by returning alive to your tent tonight. And the men and women of Troy will rejoice, seeing me return, alive, to Priam's great city. And now let's exchange precious gifts, so that all may say: They fought fiercely, but they parted in harmony and peace." So he spoke. And he gave Ajax his silver-studded sword, with its well-made sheathe and strap. And Ajax gave him his war belt of shining purple.

That night, at the banquet where we celebrated Ajax, I let them all drink and eat, and then, when I saw that they were tired, I asked the princes to listen to me. I was the oldest, and they respected my wisdom. So I said that we should ask the Trojans for a day of truce, so that we and they could gather up our dead from the battlefield. And I said that we must take advantage of that day to build a wall around the ships, a high wall, and a broad trench, to protect ourselves from an assault by the Trojans.

"*A wall? What need do we have for walls—we have shields,*" *said Diomedes. "I knock down walls, I don't build them," he said. No one liked the idea. There were even some who said, "Think how Achilles will boast when he discovers*

that without him we are so afraid that we shut ourselves
behind a wall." They laughed. But the truth is that they were
young, and the young have an old idea of war. Honor, beauty,
heroism. Like the fight between Hector and Ajax: two princes
who first try savagely to kill each other and then exchange
gifts. I was too old to believe in those things still. We won that
war by means of a huge wooden horse, filled with soldiers. We
won by a trick, not by an open, fair, honorable fight. And this
they, the young men, never liked. But I was old. Odysseus was
old. We knew that the long war we were fighting was old, and
that it would be won in a day by those who were able to fight
it in a new way.

That night we went to sleep without making a decision,
and when we woke we received a delegation from the Trojans.
Idaeus came to us and said that since the Trojans had taken
up the fight again, after the encounter between Paris and
Menelaus, and had broken the sacred pact, they were now
willing to give us our due by returning all the treasures that
Paris had carried off with Helen of Argos. Not the woman but
the treasures, yes. And he said that to those they would add
splendid gifts, to compensate us for the treachery. They were
afraid that the gods would not forgive their perfidy, you see?

Diomedes rose and said, "Not even if they gave us back
Helen in flesh and blood would we stop, my friends. Even a
fool could understand that the end of Troy is near." And we all
applauded; at that moment we felt that he was right. So
Agamemnon answered Idaeus that we rejected the offer. And
then he agreed to a truce of one day, so that we and the Trojans could gather our dead and consign them to the flames in
accordance with custom. And so it was.

A strange day of war. On the great plain, beneath the sun
that lighted up the land, went Achaeans and Trojans, mingled

together, looking for their own dead. They leaned over the fouled bodies, with water washed away the blood in order to identify the faces, and then, weeping, loaded them onto carts. Silently, with grieving hearts, they heaped the bodies on the pyres, and stood there watching as the leaping flames burned those who, until the day before, had fought at their side.

When the sun began to set, I gathered a band of Achaeans around the funeral pyre and had them construct the wall, the hated wall, with high, secure towers and broad gates so that our men could go in and out. I had them build it all the way around the ships. And I had them dig a deep trench in front of the wall to keep the Trojan chariots away. And only when it was finished did we withdraw to the tents to take the gift of sleep. During the night Zeus hurled terrible thunder from the sky, and it was a sound of disaster that left us pale with fear.

At dawn the next day we took our meal quickly and put on our armor. The Trojans emerged from the city and came toward us in an immense tumult. In the middle of the plain the two armies clashed in a fury of shields, spears, and bronze armor, of groans and shouts, of the sorrow of the killed and the triumph of the killers, while the earth was stained with blood. From dawn until noon the blows flew on one side and the other, but when the sun was high in the middle of the sky, then the fate of the battle smiled on the Trojans. Around me I saw our men begin to retreat, and then flee. I, too, thought of turning back in my chariot, like the others, but an arrow shot by Paris struck one of my horses in his forehead: he reared up in pain, then fell to the ground, upsetting the other two. With my sword I cut the traces loose from him and was about to call back the other horses when I saw Hector in his chariot speeding toward me in the fray. I was a dead man. I saw Odysseus not far from me. Even he was fleeing, so I shouted, "Odysseus, where are you going? Do you want to be killed by a spear in your back? You coward, come and help me!" But patient, glorious Odysseus couldn't hear me, and continued heading toward the ships.

It was Diomedes who came to save me. He arrived quickly in his chariot and pulled me up with him. I took the reins and urged the horses toward Hector. And when we were close enough, Diomedes hurled his spear with all his strength. When I saw that it had missed, I understood that fate was against us and it was better to escape. "Escape? Me?" said Diomedes. "And then let Hector go around boasting that Diomedes ran away from him?" *As I said, the young love glory, and so they lose wars.* "Diomedes, even if he says it, no one will believe him, because people believe the winner, not the loser." And I turned the horses in flight amid the turmoil, with the voice of Hector fading behind us, shouting insults.

We retreated to the trench and there we stopped. Hector was driving us back with his whole army, the plain was teeming with soldiers and chariots and horses. Agamemnon was shouting, urging on the Achaeans, and all the heroes fought hard, one beside the other. I remember that Teucer, the archer, hid behind the shield of Ajax, and when Ajax lowered the shield he took aim and let fly into the crowd of Trojans. He didn't miss a shot. The Trojans fell, one after the other, struck by his arrows. We shouted at him to take Hector, to aim at him. "I can't hit him, that mad dog," he said. Twice he had tried, twice missed, and he didn't have time to try again, for Hector was on him and hit him in the shoulder with a rock. The bow flew out of his hands; he fell to the ground. Ajax sheltered him with his shield, and two men managed to grab him and carry him off, far from Hector's fury.

We fought but we couldn't contain them. They pushed us

into the trench and then against the wall, while Hector never stopped shouting, "They think they can hold us back with a wall, but our chariots will fly over that wall and we won't stop until we reach the ships and fire consumes them!" Nothing could save us.

The sun saved us. It sank into Ocean, bringing night upon the fertile earth. In anger the Trojans watched it set. In joy, ourselves. Even war is obedient to the night.

We withdrew behind the wall, into our tents, in front of the ships. But Hector, for the first time in nine long years of war, didn't lead his army back inside the walls of the city. He ordered his men to camp there, at the wall. From the city he had oxen and fat sheep brought, and sweet wine and bread and wood for the blazing fires. The wind bore the odor of sacrifices. *And we, who had come from far away to lay siege to a city, became a city under siege.* All night, right before our eyes, the fires of the proud Trojans burned by the thousand. They shone the way the moon and stars shine at night under the open sky, illuminating the mountain peaks and valleys and warming the shepherd's heart with gladness. In the glow of the flames we saw the shadows of the Trojans moving in the night, waiting for Aurora on her beautiful throne.

ACHILLES

Five of them came. Odysseus first of all. Then the great warrior Ajax and Phoenix, loved by Zeus. And two heralds, Odius and Eurybates. I was in my tent, playing the lyre. It was a precious lyre—beautifully made, with a silver bridge—that I had chosen from among the spoils, and I was playing because it comforted my heart to play and sing of the adventures of heroes. Beside me Patroclus listened in silence. Then they arrived. They had been well chosen: among all the Achaeans they were most dear to me. "Friends," I said, and had them sit around me on couches covered with purple carpets. I sent Patroclus to get more wine, and he brought wine, and meat and bread.

So we feasted in my tent together, and only at the end Odysseus, who was sitting just across from me, raised a cup of wine and said, "Hail, Achilles, divine prince. Your banquet is sumptuous, but, sadly, we have not come here for your food and wine. An immense disaster threatens us, and we are afraid. If you don't take up your weapons, it will be difficult to save the ships. The proud Trojans and their allies are encamped right at the wall that we built for our defense. They have lighted a thousand fires and say they will not stop until they reach our black ships. Hector is raging, he fears neither men nor gods, he is possessed by a brutal fury. He says that he is only waiting for dawn to attack and set fire to our ships and, in the smoke, slaughter the Achaeans. He will do it, Achilles. I know, in the depths of my heart, that he will do it, and we'll all die here, in Troy, far from our homes. But if you want, there is still time to save the Achaeans before that irreparable evil, for us and also for you. My friend, do you remember the day when Peleus, your father, watched you leave at Agamemnon's side? 'The gods will give you strength,' he said to you, 'but you must restrain your proud heart. To be gentle—that is to be strong. Stay away from quarrels and arguments, and the Achaeans, young and old, will honor you.' Thus he spoke, but you have forgotten.

"Hear me now. Let me tell you, one by one, about the gifts that Agamemnon has promised if you'll set aside your anger—precious gifts, if only you'll give up your anger; splendid gifts, if only you'll forget your anger. Seven tripods never touched by fire, ten talents of gold, twenty shining bowls, twelve strong, swift stallions that have won countless races. Agamemnon will give you seven women from Lesbos skilled in handiwork, the same seven he chose for himself the day you destroyed the well-built city of Lesbos for him. They were the most beautiful: he will give them to you. And along with them he will give you Briseis, whom he took from you one day, and he will swear solemnly that he has never shared his bed with her, and has not loved her the way men and women love. All this you will have, and right away, here. And then if destiny allows us to destroy the great city of Priam, you may step forward, when the spoils are divided, and load your ship with gold and bronze, as much as you want, and twenty Trojan women, the most beautiful you can find, with the exception of Helen of Argos. And if, finally, we return to Argos, in the fertile land of Achaia, Agamemnon wants you to marry one of his three daughters, who are waiting for him now in his shining palace: you can choose the one you want and bring her to the home of Peleus, without offering any marriage gift. Agamemnon, rather, will give you pleasing gifts, more than any father has ever given to his daughter. He will give you seven of his richest cities—Cardamyle, Enope, Hire, sacred Pherae, Anthea with its green meadows, beautiful Aepea, and Pedasus lush with vineyards—all cities near the sea, all inhabited by men rich in oxen and lambs who will honor you as a god and will pay you, their king, huge tributes. All this he will give you, if you will put aside your anger. And if you can't, because Agamemnon is too hateful to you and his gifts are insupportable, then at least have pity on us, who today are suffering, and tomorrow will honor you as a god. It's the right moment to challenge Hector and kill him: he is possessed by a tremendous fury, and, with his conviction that he is the best, he won't run away. Wouldn't the glory be immense, Achilles?"

Godlike son of Laertes, sharp-witted Odysseus, it's better if I speak plainly and say what I think, and what will be: that way we can avoid sitting here talking pointlessly. There is not a single Achaean on earth who can persuade me to put aside my anger. Agamemnon can't do it, and neither can you. What advantage is there for a man who fights constantly, without respite, against any enemy? Fate is the same for the brave man and the coward, the same honor goes to the strong and the weak, and death comes equally to the man who does nothing and the one who is busy. After suffering so much, risking my life at every moment in the heart of battle, I am left with nothing. As a bird carries to her young the food she has obtained, but for herself it has been only trouble, so I have spent many sleepless nights, and many days fighting enemies on a bloody battlefield. With my ships I came to twelve cities and destroyed them. And traveling through the fertile land of Troy, I came to eleven more and destroyed them. I carried off vast treasure and gave everything to Agamemnon, the son of Atreus; and he, who stayed in safety in his tent, near the ships, accepted it. Much he kept for himself, some he distributed to the others. To kings and heroes and chiefs he always awarded a prize of honor, and they all still have theirs, but not me: from me he took mine. Agamemnon took away the woman I loved and now she sleeps with him. Let him keep her, and enjoy himself.

But why should we fight for him? Why did he assemble an army and lead it here? Was it not for fair-haired Helen? Well? Is it only the sons of Atreus who love their women? No, every wise and noble man loves his woman and takes care of her, as I with all my heart loved mine, no matter that she was a slave of war. He took her away from me, stole my prize; now I know what kind of man he is, and he will not deceive me another time. Don't try to convince me, Odysseus; think instead about how to save the ships from fire. You've done many things already without me—you built the wall, and beside the wall you dug a wide, deep trench lined with stakes. But you won't stop Hector that way. While I was fighting with you, he didn't venture far from his walls. He stayed close to the Scaean gates, and when he was feeling brave he pushed out as far as the oak. That was where he challenged me that day—

do you remember, Odysseus? He and I, one against the other.
He escaped with his life by a miracle. But now . . . now I have
no desire to fight him. Tomorrow, if you want, if it matters to
you, look toward the sea: at dawn, you'll see my ships plowing
the Hellespont, the men bent over their oars. And if the glorious god who shakes the earth grants us a good journey, after
three days I will reach the fertile land of Phthia. All I possess I
left in order to come and fight here, at the walls of Troy. I will
return, bringing with me gold and purple bronze and gleaming
iron and beautiful women, and everything that I won here:
everything except Briseis, because he who gave her to me has
taken her away from me.

Go to Agamemnon and tell him what I've said to you, and
do it publicly, in front of everyone, so that the other Achaeans
may understand what sort of man he is, and take care not to
be deceived themselves. I tell you, however shameless he is, he
will never have the courage to look me in the eye. And I will
not come to his aid, either by fighting or by giving counsel. I've
had enough—he can go to disaster. There's nothing I can do if
he acts foolishly. I care nothing for him, and I despise his gifts:
even if he were to give me ten, twenty times what he has, even
if he offered me as many gifts as there are grains of sand, even
then he would not soften my heart. First he must pay, completely, for the terrible injury he has done me. And I will not
marry one of his daughters, not even if she were as beautiful as
Aphrodite or as wise as Athena. Hand her in marriage to
someone else, maybe someone more powerful than I, someone
of her rank . . . If the gods save me, if I return home, my father
will choose a wife for me. I want to go home, I want to return,
to enjoy in peace what is mine, with a woman, a wife, beside
me. All the treasures that Troy conceals behind its walls, however vast, are not worth what life is worth. Oxen and fat sheep

can be stolen, with gold one can buy one's fill of horses and precious tripods. But life—it can't be stolen, can't be bought. It goes out of your throat and doesn't go back in. My mother, one day, told me what my destiny will be: if I stay here, fighting beside the walls of Troy, I will never return but will have eternal glory. And if instead I go home, to my native land, there will be no glory for me, but I will have a long life, before death, walking slowly, comes for me. I say to you, too: go home. We will never see the fall of Troy.

Return to your tents and take my message to the Achaean chiefs. Tell them to find some other way to save the ships and the army. I can't help them. Tell them that I remain steadfast in my anger.

I spoke, and they were all silent: disturbed and surprised by my refusal.

As I said, Phoenix was with them, the old man Phoenix. My father had ordered him to go with me to the walls of Troy. I was a boy, I knew nothing of war or assemblies. My father spoke to Phoenix, told him to stay with me and teach me everything. And he obeyed. He was like a second father to me. And now I found him on the other side, with Odysseus and Ajax, and it was absurd. So before he returned with them to Agamemnon, I said to him, "Stay with me, Phoenix, sleep in my tent tonight." I said to him that the next day he could leave with me. I said that I wouldn't insist, but if he wanted, he could leave with me and return to our homeland.

"Glorious Achilles," he answered, "if you are really thinking of returning, how could I, my child, stay on alone, without you? For years I have loved you with all my heart. I made you what you are. Do you remember? You didn't want to go with anyone else to the banquets, and even at home you wouldn't eat unless I took you on my knee and fed you, cutting the meat for you and pouring the wine. You were a child. Capricious. How many times you soiled my tunic, spitting out your wine. But whatever the trouble or hardship, I was happy if it was for you, because you are the son I'll never have. And today, if anyone can save me from unhappiness, it's you. Soften your proud heart, Achilles. Don't be so harsh. Even the gods are moved, sometimes, and they are a thousand times as brave and strong as you. They let themselves be appeased by the prayers of men, who, to redeem their errors, offer supplications, libations, and gifts. Prayers are the daughters of Zeus. They are lame, and squint-eyed, and wrinkled, but they struggle to follow in the footsteps of our errors to offer redemption. They are the daughters of Zeus: respect them. If you reject them, they will return to their father and ask him to persecute you. Agamemnon prays that you will let go of your anger: honor that prayer. Don't let your demon anger control you. Come and defend the ships. What use will it be to save them when they are already in flames?"

Phoenix.

Good old Phoenix.

Don't love Agamemnon if you don't want to be hated by me, who love you. Don't whine to defend him. Love those whom I love and be king with me, and share my honor with me. Let the others go back to the Achaeans with my message. You stay and sleep here, and tomorrow we'll decide whether to return home on our ships.

At that point Ajax turned to Odysseus and said, "Let's go, we'll get nowhere like this. The heart of Achilles is savage and full of pride, and he is incapable of hearing the friendship we offered him. The Achaeans are waiting for an answer. Let's bring it to them, even if it is a cruel, foolish answer."

There, that's a good idea, Ajax. Go back to Agamemnon and tell him on my behalf that I will return to battle when Hector reaches my ships, not yours. Here, at my tent, I will stop him, and not before.

They left. And I could imagine them, the Achaean princes, gathered that night around a fire, hearing my answer, astonished. I could see them return, one by one, each into his own tent, in silence, waiting for the rosy light of Aurora and begging for the gift of sleep.

DIOMEDES · ODYSSEUS

DIOMEDES

We all slept beside our ships, overcome by weariness. But not Agamemnon. He was awake. He went on thinking, and the more he thought, the more his heart trembled in his breast. He looked toward the plain of Troy and what he saw was the Trojans' fires, burning by the thousand: they were so close that he could hear the voices of the soldiers and the sound of flutes and pipes.

ODYSSEUS

So Agamemnon rose in anguish. He dressed. He threw over his shoulders the tawny skin of a lion that, broad and full, fell to his feet, and he took his spear and went in search of Nestor. Maybe he had an idea of how to get out of that trap. He was the oldest, the wisest. Maybe together they would think of a plan to save the Achaeans. He went looking for him. In the darkness—it was still night—he met his brother, Menelaus. He couldn't sleep, either. He was wandering around, frightened, thinking of the suffering to which he—he—had condemned all the Achaeans. He was armed, the spear in his hand, the helmet on his head, and the skin of a spotted leopard over his shoulders. They looked at each other, the two brothers.

DIOMEDES

"What are you doing up, and armed?" Menelaus asked. "Are you looking for someone to send into the Trojan camp, to spy on the enemy's moves? It won't be easy to find anyone."

"I'm trying to find a plan to save the Achaeans," Agamemnon answered. "What Hector did today I have never seen done by a man. We won't soon forget the evil he inflicted on us. I'm afraid that our men won't remain faithful for long if they continue to suffer like this. Listen to me: you run beside the ships and call Ajax and Idomeneus. And as you go, tell the men to wake, and treat them kindly, don't be overbearing. I am going to Nestor. I'll ask him to come to the guard post and talk to the soldiers, they'll trust him."

ODYSSEUS

Menelaus hurried off, and Agamemnon went to Nestor's tent. He found him lying on a soft bed. Beside him he kept his weapons, the shield, the two spears, the shining helmet. And also that bright-colored war belt that he always wore when he went into battle, leading his men. Although he was old, he wasn't bent by age, and would still fight. "Who are you, there in the dark?" said Nestor, raising his head. "Don't come any closer. Tell me who you are."

"It's Agamemnon, Nestor. I'm here, walking around in the darkness, because sweet sleep won't close my eyes while thoughts of the war and the sufferings of the Achaeans torment me. I am afraid for us, Nestor. My heart is bursting and my knees are weak. Come with me to the guard post. Let's go and make sure the men are watching properly: the enemy is so close and could attack again, tonight."

"Agamemnon, glorious son of Atreus, lord of men, why are you afraid?" answered the old man. "Hector won't always win, and in fact I say to you that he will endure sufferings much greater than the ones he made us endure today: we must only wait for Achilles to return to battle. But come, we'll go to the guard post. Let's also wake the others, Diomedes, Odysseus, Ajax . . ." He wrapped himself in a large, heavy purple cloak made of fine wool and took his spear. Together they went to find the others. They came to me, first of all.

"Who is there in the dark? What are you looking for?"

"Don't be afraid, Odysseus. It's Nestor, and with me is Agamemnon. Get up and come with us. We must get together and take counsel, and decide whether to flee or stay and fight."

DIOMEDES

They found me lying out on the hide of an ox, still armed, and surrounded by my men.

"Diomedes, wake up! How can you be sleeping with the Trojans camped so close to our ships?"

"Nestor, you are really something. Do you never sleep? Isn't there someone younger you could send to wake the Achaeans one by one? But you are never tired, eh?"

Finally we all reached the guard post. There no one was

sleeping, the guards were armed and alert. Keeping a constant watch on the plain, they waited, listening for signs of the Trojans. Nestor looked at them proudly. "Go on watching like that, my sons: don't let sleep overcome you, and our enemies won't have a chance to laugh at us." Then he crossed the trench and sat down on the ground, in a clear space where there were no bodies of fallen men. It was more or less the point where Hector had stopped when he saw night descending. We all followed him there, and sat down.

ODYSSEUS

"Friends," said Nestor, "is there any one of you bold and confident enough to penetrate the Trojans' camp and capture someone or listen to what they're saying, to find out if they intend to go on fighting here, at our ships, or are thinking of returning to defend themselves within the walls of their city? If anyone could do such a thing and return safe and sound, his glory among men will be great. All the princes will give him rich gifts, and his enterprise will be talked of at every banquet, every feast, forever."

DIOMEDES

"I am both brave and bold," I said. "I can do it. Give me a companion and I will do it. If there are two of us, I will be even bolder. And two heads are better than one." Then they all offered; all the princes said they were willing to follow me. Agamemnon looked at me and said that I must choose. He said also that I mustn't think of offending anyone, that I should choose freely. It didn't matter even if I chose a man who was not of noble birth—no one would be offended. He was thinking of Menelaus, you see. He was afraid that I would choose his little brother. But I said: I want Odysseus, because he is brave and he is also clever. If he comes with me, we'd manage to escape even blazing fire, because he knows how to use his brain.

ODYSSEUS

He began to praise me in front of the others, but I made him stop. I said it was better to get going: the stars had made much progress in their course, and dawn was near. What was left of the night was all we had.

We put on our tremendous weapons. Thrasymedes offered Diomedes a two-edged sword and a shield. Meriones gave me bow, quiver, and sword. We both put on helmets of leather: no bronze, no gleam that might betray us in the darkness. When we left, we heard in the darkness the cry of a heron. I thought it was a sign from heaven and that this time, too, Athena, the shining goddess, was with me. "Let me return safe and sound to the ships, friendly goddess, and help me to carry out an undertaking that the Trojans will never forget." We hurried silently through the black night like a pair of lions, walking amid piles of corpses and heaps of weapons, and pools of black blood.

DIOMEDES

Suddenly Odysseus says to me, "Diomedes, Diomedes, do you hear that sound? There's someone there, someone coming from the Trojan camp and running toward our ships. Be quiet. We'll let him go and when he gets closer we'll jump him, all right?"

"All right," I say.

"And if by chance he tries to run away, we'll cut off his escape so he can't turn back. We'll drive him away from home. Let's go."

ODYSSEUS

We left the road and slipped into the fields, which were littered with dead bodies. And immediately we saw the man running right in front of us. We followed him. He heard us and stopped. Maybe he thought we, too, were Trojans, who had been sent to help him. But when we arrived within a spear's throw, he realized who we were and ran. And we were behind him.

DIOMEDES

Like two hunting dogs, stalking their prey without pause through the thick of the wood, in pursuit of a fleeing deer or hare . . . The problem was that he was now about to reach the wall, fall right in the hands of our sentries. And this no, you know? After that whole chase, then to be cheated of my prey, no. So, still running, I shouted, "Stop or I'll take you out with my spear, I swear, stop or you're dead!" and I threw the spear, aiming a little high. I didn't want to kill him, I wanted to make him stop. The spear passes over his right shoulder and he . . . stops. It always works, that trick.

ODYSSEUS

He stammered, his teeth chattering in fear. "Don't kill me, my father will pay whatever ransom. He is rich in gold, and bronze, and well-wrought iron." He entreated us and wept. His name was Dolon, the son of Eumedes.

DIOMEDES

I, for myself, would have killed him. But as I said, Odysseus was the one who used his brain. So I stand there and Odysseus starts to interrogate him. "Stop thinking about death and tell me instead what you were doing out here, so far from your camp. Were you stealing armor from the corpses, or are you a spy sent by Hector to our ships to discover our secrets?" He wouldn't stop crying. "It's Hector's fault, he tricked me. He promised me the chariot and horses of Achilles, I swear, and in exchange he asked me to go to your ships and spy on you. He wanted to know if there were sentinels guarding the camp or if by now you were thinking of flight, or were sleeping from the exhaustion and suffering of your defeat." Odysseus smiled. "The horses of Achilles? This is what you want, nothing less than the horses of Achilles? Good luck: it won't be easy to keep them under control and drive them, for a simple man like you. Achilles himself has trouble, and he is half god."

ODYSSEUS

We made him talk. We wanted to know where Hector was, where he kept his weapons and his horses, and what he had in mind—whether to attack again or retreat into the city. Dolon was afraid. He told everything, concealed nothing. He said that Hector was taking counsel with all his wisest men near the tomb of Ilus. And he described to us the camp and how the Trojans and their allies were arrayed. He named them one by one and told us where they were, and who was on watch and who was sleeping. Finally he burst out, "Stop asking me questions. If what you want is to infiltrate and attack, then take the Thracians. They arrived just a short time ago, and are isolated, unprotected, on the flank. And Rhesus, the king, is in the middle. He fights with weapons of shining gold, marvelous to see, the arms of a god, not a man. I've seen his horses, big, handsome, whiter than snow, and swift as the wind; his chariot is adorned with gold and silver. Attack him. And now take me to the ships and tie me up there, until your return—then you'll know if I've lied to you or not."

DIOMEDES

He thought he'd get out of it that way, you see? "You think you're going to get out of it that way, Dolon? Forget it. You've given us a lot of useful information, thank you. But the fact is that, unfortunately, you are in my hands. If I let you go, you know what will happen? Tomorrow I'll find you here spying again or, worse, I'll find you facing me in battle, armed, and with the idea of killing me. If, however, I kill you now, tomorrow none of those things will happen." And with my sword I cut off his head, cleanly. He was still talking with that mouth, and reaching his hand toward me in entreaty, and I cut off his head with my sword and watched it roll in the dirt. I see again as if it were now Odysseus picking up the body and offering it to Athena—"This is for you, predator goddess"—and then he hangs it on a tamarisk and ties reeds and flowering branches around it, so that, returning after our foray, we can find it and bring it to the camp, our trophy!

ODYSSEUS

We ran among the corpses and the abandoned weapons and the black blood everywhere, until we came to the camp of the Thracians. Dolon hadn't lied. They were sleeping, overcome by exhaustion. They had placed their weapons on the ground beside them, all in order, in three rows. Each warrior had two horses nearby. Right in the middle, Rhesus was sleeping. His magnificent horses were tied by their reins to the rim of the chariot.

DIOMEDES

Then Odysseus says to me, "Diomedes, look, that's him, Rhesus, and those are the horses Dolon was talking about. It's time to use the weapons you brought with you. You take care of the men, I'll take care of the horses." So he says to me. And I raise my sword and start killing. They were all sleeping, you see? I was like a lion who meets a flock without its shepherd, and pounces in the midst of it, raging. I kill them one after another, blood everywhere, twelve of them I kill. And every time one dies I see Odysseus take him by the feet and get him out of the way—now think what a brain, that man. He moved the bodies, hid them, because he had already thought of Rhesus's horses, which had just arrived and weren't used to bodies and blood, and so, think what a brain, he cleared a path so that he could drive them away and they wouldn't get agitated finding a dead man under their hooves, or the red of blood in their eyes. Odysseus . . . well, in the end I get to Rhesus. He was sleeping, and dreaming. He was having a nightmare, he was talking and tossing, I think he had dreamed of me—I'm sure of it, he was dreaming of Diomedes, son of Tydeus, grandson of Oeneus—and his dream killed him, with my sword I killed him—while Odysseus frees the horses with their thick hooves and urges them on, spurring them on with his bow, because he doesn't have a whip, nothing. To get them going he has to use his bow, imagine, and with that he drives them off and then whistles to me from a distance, because he wants to get out of there as soon as possible. He whistles to me but, I don't know, there's the chariot, Rhesus's fantastic gold and silver chariot. I could grab it by the pole or just lift it up— I could do that, but Odysseus calls me. If I stay I'll have to kill some more and then I might not get out alive, but still, I would like to go on killing. I see Odysseus leaping onto the horse, right onto its back, holds the reins in his hand, looks at me. To hell with the chariot, to hell with the Thracians, out of there, before it's too late. Running, I reach Odysseus, I jump onto the horse's back and we go, he and I, swiftly to the swift ships of the Danaans.

ODYSSEUS

When we reached the point where we had killed the spy, the man named Dolon, I stopped the horses. Diomedes dismounted, picked up the bloody corpse, and handed it to me. Then he got back on the horse and we galloped to the trench and the wall and our ships. When we arrived, they all crowded around us, they shouted, they grasped our hands, they wanted to know everything. Nestor, the old man, you could see he had been afraid that he would never see us again. "Odysseus, tell us, where did you get these horses? Did you steal them from the Trojans, or did a god give them to you? They are like rays of sun, and I, who am always in the midst of the Trojans—

because even though I'm an old man I don't sit idly by the ships—well, I've never seen horses like that in battle." And I told him, because this is my fate, and I kept nothing back, about the spy, and Rhesus, and the thirteen men killed by Diomedes, and the magnificent horses. Finally we all returned through the trench and I went with Diomedes to his tent. We tied the horses to the manger beside his horses and gave them sweet grain. Then we jumped into the sea, he and I, into the water to wash away the blood and sweat from our legs, from our thighs, from our backs. And after the waves of the sea washed us, we went into the polished baths to rest and comfort our hearts. Washed and anointed with olive oil, we sat at the banquet, finally, drinking sweet wine.

DIOMEDES

Odysseus placed the bloody corpse of the spy on the stern of his ship. It is for you, Athena, predator goddess.

PATROCLUS

My name is Patroclus, the son of Menoetius. Years ago, because I killed a boy like me, I had to leave my native land, and with my father I came to Phthia, where the wise and valiant Peleus reigned. The king had a son: his name was Achilles. Strange tales circulated about him. That his mother was a goddess. That he was reared without knowing woman's milk, nourished on the entrails of lions and the marrow of bears. That he would become the fighter without whom Troy would never be conquered. Today his bones are mingled with mine, buried on the white island. His death belongs to him. Mine began at dawn after the night when Odysseus and Diomedes stole the shining horses of Rhesus. At the first light of day, Agamemnon assembled the army for battle. He ordered the charioteers to keep the chariots on this side of the trench, in orderly ranks, and sent the men, on foot, across to get ready to fight on the other side. All obeyed except us Myrmidons, because Achilles didn't want us to fight. I stayed in front of our tent. On the plain opposite us I saw the Trojans gather close around their commanders. I remember Hector: he appeared and disappeared among his soldiers, like a glittering star amid the clouds of a dark night sky. *All that I saw that day, from afar, and that I heard of, I want you to hear, now, if you wish to understand the death I wanted to die.*

The two armies clashed. The men advanced without fear and without thought of flight, with the inexorable calm of a thousand reapers who methodically follow their row along the field and mow down what is in their path. Throughout the dawn men fell, and weapons sparkled, and neither of the two armies prevailed. But when the light of the sun rose above the horizon, then, suddenly, the Achaeans broke the Trojan ranks. Agamemnon led them, with a strength never before seen, as if this were to be his day of glory. Advancing, he killed whoever he came upon, first Bienor, then Oileus, and two sons of Priam, Isus and Antiphus. When Pisander and intrepid Hippolochus appeared before him, standing in their chariot, one beside the other, he dragged them to the ground and leaped on them, like a lion who in the deer's lair sinks his teeth in her young and kills them. They begged him to let them live: they said that their father, Antilochus, would pay immense riches in ransom. But Agamemnon said, "If you are really sons of Antilochus, then pay for the crime of your father, who in the council of the Trojans, when my brother came to reclaim his wife, voted to kill him and send him home dead." And he struck Pisander in the chest with his spear. And with his sword he cut off Hippolochus's arms, and then his head, and sent him rolling like a trunk through the dust of battle.

Where the fray was thickest he charged, and behind him came the Achaeans, cutting off the heads of the Trojans. Men on foot killed men on foot, men in chariots killed men in chariots, and the horses with their proud heads ran wild, pulling empty chariots and mourning their drivers, who now lay on the ground, more loved by the vultures than by their wives. As far as the tomb of Ilus, in the middle of the plain, Agamemnon drove the Trojans, and then farther, forcing them back to their walls, to the Scaean gates: there he pursued, running and shouting, his hands stained with blood. The Trojans fled: they seemed like cows that have caught the scent of a lion and gone mad. Hector had to jump down from his chariot, shouting and urging his men on. For a while they stopped fleeing and drew up again in order. The Achaeans closed their ranks. Again the two armies were face-to-face, looking into each other's eyes.

And again the first to charge was Agamemnon. He attacked Iphidamas, the son of Antenor, a big valiant man who had grown up in the fertile land of Thrace. Agamemnon hurled his spear but missed, and the bronze tip ended nowhere. Then Iphidamas, in turn, gripped his spear and threw it, and struck Agamemnon: the point entered under his breastplate and went into his belt. Iphidamas bore down with all his strength, so that it would penetrate the leather, into the flesh. But Agamemnon's belt had silver studs, and the silver wouldn't yield: with all his might Iphidamas tried, but he couldn't pierce that belt. Then Agamemnon got his hands on the spear and, raging like a lion, tore it away from Iphidamas and, having disarmed him, struck him right in the neck with his sword and took away his life. Thus, unhappy man, he fell, and slept a sleep of bronze. There was his brother, not far away, his older brother. His name was Coon. He saw Iphidamas fall and a tremendous grief clouded his eyes. Then he went toward Agamemnon, but without being seen, and took him by surprise, striking with his spear just under the elbow:

the shining tip of the shaft pierced the flesh. Agamemnon shuddered but didn't run: he saw Coon dragging away the body of his brother, holding it by the ankles, and he hurled himself at him and, driving his spear in under the shield, hit him. Coon fell on the body of his brother. And Agamemnon, standing over him, lifted the man's head and with his sword cut it off. Thus the two sons of Antenor, one beside the other, fulfilled their destiny and descended to the house of Hades.

Agamemnon went on fighting amid the fray, but his wound bled, and the pain became intolerable. Finally he called to his driver for help and, climbing into the chariot, ordered him to spur the horses to the hollow ships. Sorrowing in his heart, he cried to the Achaeans, with all the strength he had left, "Fight for me and defend our ships." The charioteer whipped the horses with their fine manes, and, leaping forward, their breasts covered with foam and stained with dust, they took flight and carried the suffering king far from the battle.

"Trojans, the man who fought hardest today is gone!" Hector cried. "Now it's our turn for glory. Spur your horses and attack the Achaeans. The greatest triumph awaits us." And he drew them all behind him, charging into the battle like a storm wind that beats down upon the violet sea. It was impressive to see, as the heads of the Achaean fighters rolled, one after the other, under his sword. Asaeus died first, and then Autonous and Opites, and Dolops, the son of Clytius, and Opheltius, and Agelaus, Aesymnus, Oros, and valiant Hipponous, and many others without name, in the tumult. Heads rolled the way huge waves roll during a storm at sea, when the spray boils up under the raging wind.

It was the end. It seemed the end, for us. As the Achaeans were fleeing, Odysseus stopped and, seeing Diomedes not far from him, cried, "Diomedes, what in the world is happening? Have we forgotten our strength and courage? Come and fight beside me. Surely you don't want to flee?"

"I won't flee," Diomedes answered, and with a thrust of his spear knocked Thymbraeus out of his chariot and killed him. "I won't flee, but without the help of heaven we will not get out of here alive." They began fighting alongside each other, like two proud boars, furiously charging against a pack of hounds. The Achaeans, seeing them, took courage, and for a moment the fate of battle seemed to change. But Hector, too, saw them, and with a shout he rushed through the ranks toward them. "Disaster is heading for us," Diomedes said to Odysseus. "Let's stop and wait here. If it's us he wants, we'll defend ourselves." He waited until Hector was close enough and, aiming at his head, hurled his long-shadowed spear. The bronze tip struck the top of the helmet and ricocheted to the ground. Hector took a step backward and fell to his knees, stunned by the blow. And while Diomedes ran to recover his spear, Hector was able to stand up and climb into his chariot and flee into the midst of his men.

"Hector, you dog, you've managed yet again to escape death," Diomedes shouted at him. "But I tell you that the next time I will kill you, if only the gods help me the way they've helped you today." And he started killing any who came within his range. He would never have stopped except that from a distance Paris saw him: he was in the shelter of a column at the tomb of Ilus. He stretched his bow and shot. The arrow struck Diomedes in the right foot, passed through the flesh, and stuck in the ground.

"I got you, Diomedes!" Paris had come out of his hiding place and now he was shouting, and laughing. "It's just too bad I didn't rip open your stomach, so the Trojans would stop quaking before you." He laughed.

"Cowardly archer," Diomedes answered, "reckless seducer, come here and fight, instead of using your arrows from a distance. You scratched my foot and you brag about it. But look at me, I couldn't care less about your wound. It's as if a woman had struck me, or a snot-nosed kid. Didn't they teach you that the arrows of a coward are always blunt? Not my spear—when it hits it kills, women become widows, children orphans, and fathers corpses that lie rotting for the vultures." Thus he cried. And meanwhile Odysseus got between him and the Trojans to protect him. Diomedes sat on the ground and pulled the bloody arrow out of his foot. He felt the pain through his whole body. So he had to get into the chariot, with his heart full of anguish, and withdraw from the battle.

Odysseus saw him go and realized that he was alone, abandoned by his friend and all the Achaean warriors, who had fled in fear. Around him were only Trojans: they were like dogs encircling a boar that has emerged from the forest. And Odysseus was afraid. He could have run, but he didn't. He charged Deiopites and struck him. Then he killed Thoon and Eunomus and Chersidamas. With a thrust of the spear he wounded Charops, and was finishing him when his brother Socus arrived to defend him. Socus hurled his spear and the bronze tip pierced the shield of Odysseus and penetrated the armor, tearing the skin, on his side. Odysseus stepped back. He realized that he had been hit. He raised his spear. Socus had already turned and was trying to escape. Odysseus hurled it, and the bronze tip struck Socus between the shoulders and emerged from his chest. "It will not be your father and mother who close your eyes," Odysseus said. "The birds will tear them to shreds with a rapid beating of wings." Then he gripped Socus's spear in his hands and pulled it out of his flesh. He felt a tremendous pain and the blood spurted from the wound. The Trojans, too, saw him, and, urging each other on, they pressed close around him. Then Odysseus cried out. Three times, with all his strength, he cried help. Help. Help.

From far away Menelaus heard him. "It's the voice of Odysseus." Immediately he grabbed Ajax, who was beside him, and said, "That is the voice of Odysseus asking for help. Come on, let's go into the battle to save him." They found him fighting like a lion attacked by a thousand jackals, holding off death with his spear. Ajax rushed to his side and raised high his shield to protect him. And meanwhile Menelaus came and, taking him by the hand, dragged him away, toward the horses and chariots that would carry him to safety. Ajax stayed to fight, causing pandemonium among the Trojans. He killed Doryclus and then struck Pandocus and also Lysander and Pyrasus and Pylartes: he was like a river in flood, rushing down from the mountains to overflow the plain, carrying with it oaks and pines and mud, all the way to the sea. From far off, one could see his immense shield swaying in the midst of the battle. And from far off Hector saw it, as he fought on the left flank of the Achaeans, on the banks of Scamander. He saw it, and had his driver lash the horses, and headed straight toward him. The chariot sped through the battle, riding over bodies and shields; the blood sprayed up under the wheels and hooves, up to the edges of the chariot and all around. Ajax saw him coming and was afraid. In confusion, he flung the enormous shield with its seven layers of ox hide over his shoulders and began to retreat. He looked around like a hunted beast. He retreated, but slowly. He kept turning around and stopping to respond to the Trojan assaults, and again escaping, only to stop again, turn, and fight, while the spears of his enemies rained thick upon him, hungry for flesh, stabbing the shield or the ground—he was alone against all, like a lion forced to flee its own prey, like an ass patient under the children's blows.

And Achilles called me.

He was standing on the stern of his ship, and from there watching the terrible battle, that grievous defeat. He had seen Nestor's chariot flash by and, in the chariot, someone lying wounded, who seemed to him Machaon. Machaon was worth more than a hundred men. He alone knew how to draw arrows out of flesh and heal wounds with drugs that soothed the pain. So Achilles said to me, "Go to Nestor's tent, hurry, go and see if it was really Machaon, and if he is still alive and if he will die."

And I went. I ran beside the ships, swiftly, along the shore of the sea. Who could have imagined that I had begun to die?

I reached Nestor's tent. He rose from his shining chair and invited me to enter. But I didn't want to. Achilles was waiting for an answer, he wanted to know about Machaon. "Since when does Achilles have pity for wounded Achaeans?" said Nestor. "Maybe he doesn't know that the tents are full of them, on this day of defeat. Diomedes, Odysseus, Agamemnon, all wounded. Eurypylus, struck in the thigh by an arrow. And Machaon, also struck by an arrow—I just carried him out of the battle. But none of this matters to Achilles, right? Maybe he is waiting, to feel pity, waiting for the ships to burn on the shore of the sea, and for all of us to be killed, one by one . . . Then he'll shed tears . . . Friend, remember what your father said when you left, you and Achilles, for this war. He said to you, 'My son, Achilles is nobler in birth, but he is only a boy, you are older than he. Guide him, he'll listen to you.

Even though he is much stronger than you, if you give him good counsel, he'll listen to you.' Do you remember? It would seem not. Well, remind Achilles of it, if he really will listen to you. And if he continues to be obstinate in his anger, then listen to me, boy: tell him to give you his marvelous armor. You put it on and go into battle at the head of the Myrmidons. The Trojans will take you for him and in terror will abandon the fight. For a little while we'll be able to breathe: sometimes in war a pause is enough to regain courage and strength. His armor, Patroclus, have him give you his armor."

I ran off. I had to return to Achilles. And I ran off. I remember that before I got back, as I was passing the tent of Odysseus, I heard a voice calling me. I turned and saw Eurypylus, who had been carried far from the battle with an arrow sticking in one thigh. The black blood striped his leg, sweat drenched his head and shoulders. I heard his voice say, "There is no longer any escape for us." And then, softly, "Save me, Patroclus."

And I saved him. I saved them, all of them, with my courage and my folly.

SARPEDON · TELAMONIAN AJAX · HECTOR

SARPEDON

There was that trench all around the wall that the Achaeans had built to protect their ships. Hector shouted to us to cross it, but the horses didn't want to get near it. They planted their hooves and whinnied in fear. The sides were steep and the Achaeans had planted sharp stakes along the edges. To think of crossing there with our chariots was madness. Polydamas said that to Hector, told him that to go down into it was too risky, and if the Achaeans should counterattack? We would be right in the middle of the trench, trapped. It would be a slaughter. The only thing was to get out of the chariots, leave them on the far side of the trench, and attack on foot. Hector said he was right. He got out of his chariot and ordered everyone to do likewise. We lined up in five groups. Hector commanded the first, Paris the second, Helenus the third, Aeneas the fourth. The fifth was mine. We were ready to attack, but the truth was that something held us back. Still we hesitated, there on the edge of the trench.

And just at that moment an eagle appeared in the sky, flying high above us, and in its claws it was clutching an enormous snake, bloody but still alive. And at some point the snake turned and bit the eagle's chest, just at the neck; and she, transfixed by the pain, let go of her prey, almost threw it down among us, and flew away, with sharp, screeching cries. We watched that spotted snake fall, and then we saw it on the ground among us, and we all shuddered. Polydamas hurried to Hector and said, "Did you see the eagle? Just as we were about to go down into the trench she flew over us, and did you see, she had to drop her prey, she couldn't bring it to her nest, to her young. Do you know what a seer would say, Hector? That we, too, think we've caught our prey, but it will escape us. Maybe we'll reach the ships, but we won't capture them, and at that point, once we've crossed the trench, a retreat would become a massacre."

Hector looked at him furiously. "Polydamas, you're joking, or maybe you're mad. I believe in the voice of Zeus, not the flight of birds. And that voice has promised me victory. Birds . . . the only omen I believe in is the will to fight for your homeland. You are afraid, Polydamas. But don't worry: even if we all die beside that wall, you risk nothing, because you won't get there, coward that you are." And then he went forward toward the trench, leading us all.

AJAX

A terrifying wind arose: dust everywhere, swirling up against the ships. The Trojans crossed the trench and attacked our wall. They shook the merlons of the towers, they broke down the parapet, they tried to tear out the buttresses that supported the wall. We were at the top, protected behind our shields of ox hide, and striking whenever we could. Rocks flew everywhere, like flakes of snow in a winter storm. We would have done it—the wall stood up well—but then Sarpedon arrived. With his huge shield of bronze and gold, held out before him, and two spears gripped in his fists, he came upon us like a hungry lion.

SARPEDON

I was right in the middle of the crush, Glaucus was beside me. "Glaucus, are we or are we not the bravest of the Lycians, whom the rest honor and venerate? Then let's get this done, let's get over this wall. You have to die somehow, so let's do it here. At least we'll give someone his glory, or someone will give it to us." And with Glaucus and all the Lycians I attacked.

AJAX

On one of the towers the men saw them coming and called for help, but no one heard them, there was such a din. Finally they sent a messenger, who came to me and said, "Ajax, the Lycians have attacked the wall in a mass, at the tower defended by Teucer. Hurry, they need help." I set off at a run, and when I got there I saw that they were at the end of their resources. There was a big rock leaning against the parapet. I lifted it—I don't know how I had the strength; truly, it was immense— but I lifted it up and threw it down onto the heads of the Lycians. And meanwhile Teucer, with an arrow, shot Glaucus in the arm, just as he was about to get over the wall. He shot him in the arm and Glaucus slid down.

SARPEDON

He was hit, and he went and hid behind us. He didn't want some Achaean to know that he was wounded, you see? He didn't want to give anyone that glory. I was so angry I could hardly see. I was right at the top of the wall, and I gripped the parapet with both hands, using all the strength I had, and tore it away. I swear, it came off in one piece, down with the parapet. Now we would get through.

AJAX

Suddenly Sarpedon was right in front of us. He had rotated the shield around to his back to scale the wall, and now he came at us like that, unprotected. Teucer shot an arrow straight into his breast, but that man was fortunate. The arrow hit the shield's leather strap, across his chest, and stuck there.

SARPEDON

I shouted to the others, "What's wrong with you? Do I have to take this wall by myself? Where is your courage, your spirit?" And then they all piled into the breach, and there was a tremendous fight. The light shields yielded under the bronze spear points; the tower was covered with blood, both Trojan and Achaean—we attacked but couldn't get through. It was like a scale that hovers, always in balance: the Achaean side wouldn't drop. It seemed that the fight would never end, when suddenly we heard the voice of Hector shouting, "Go, let's go, to the wall, to the ships," and it was as if that voice were pushing us up, up, and over the wall . . .

AJAX

Hector was right in front of one of the gates. Nearby was a huge rock; it was lying on the ground and had a sharp, jagged point at one end. He picked it up—and I swear, it was huge; two men would have had trouble with it—but he lifted it up, lifted it high above his head. We saw him take a few steps toward the gate, and then with all his might he hurled that rock at it. The impact was such that the hinges tore away, the wood split, the bolts yielded abruptly. Rapid as the night Hector advanced into the chasm that had opened, splendid in the bronze that clothed him, two spears in his hands, his eyes burning like fire. I tell you that only a god could have stopped him at that moment. He turned to his men and shouted to them to go, go through the wall. We saw them coming, charging through the ruined gate or climbing over the wall at every point. All was lost. We could only flee, and we fled toward our ships, toward all that remained to us.

AJAX

From his tent, Nestor, the old man, saw us fleeing, with the shattered wall behind us and the Trojans at our heels, pushing us toward the ships like a flame, like a storm. He hurried to find the other kings who were lying wounded in their tents— Diomedes, Odysseus, Agamemnon. Together they observed the battlefield, leaning on their spears, their hearts constricted by grief.

Agamemnon spoke first. "Hector promised. He said that he wouldn't stop before he set fire to the ships. And now here he is, he's coming. I fear that all the Achaeans are angry with me, each one an Achilles, and sooner or later they'll refuse to keep fighting."

Nestor gazed at that desperate retreat. "The wall we hoped would be an indestructible defense for us and our ships has crumbled," he said. "It's a sad fact, and not even a god could change it. Now we must think what to do. Our men are being routed, and in that tremendous chaos they are simply trying to escape slaughter. We have to do something. But I don't think we can fight ourselves: you are all wounded, I am old. We can't do it."

Then Agamemnon said, "If we can't fight, we'll flee." He said it himself, the king of kings. "These are my orders. We'll wait for night, and then, with the favoring darkness, we'll put to sea in the ships and go. It's not dishonorable to avoid a disaster. And if the only way to be saved is to flee, flee is what we must do."

Odysseus looked at him fiercely. "What sort of words escaped your lips, unlucky Agamemnon? Give orders like that to someone else, but don't give them to us, who are men of honor, and whose destiny it is to wind the thread of bitter wars from youth to old age, until we die. You want to abandon Troy, after we have suffered so much for it? Be quiet, so that the Achaeans don't hear you. Those are words that should never come to the lips of a man who holds in his hands the scepter of command."

Agamemnon lowered his gaze. "You strike me to the heart, Odysseus, with your words. And it's true, I don't want to order you to flee if you don't want to. But what else can we do? Is there anyone, young or old, who has an idea? I am ready to listen."

Then up jumped Diomedes, who was the youngest of us all. "Listen to me, Agamemnon. I know that I am younger than you, but put aside envy or rancor and listen to me. Even if we are wounded, let's return to battle. We'll keep away from the heart of the fray, but let ourselves be seen there. We have to be seen, the men will see us and recover their courage and their will to fight." He was the youngest, but in the end they listened to him, because they could do nothing else—and because their destiny, ours, was to wind the thread of bitter wars from youth to old age, until death.

SARPEDON

In a mass we charged behind Hector. As a stone falling from a mountain peak rolls and ricochets, making the woods echo as it passes, and doesn't stop until it reaches the plain, so that man wished to reach the sea, the ships, the tents of the Achaeans, sowing death. Around him raged war—war that annihilates men, that bristles with sharp-pointed spears. We advanced from every direction, dazzled by flashes of brilliance from shining helmets, glittering armor, and gleaming shields. How could one forget that brilliance? But I tell you: there is no heart so bold it could look at that beauty without being frightened by it.

And we were frightened, fascinated but frightened, as Hector led us forward, as if he saw nothing but those ships ahead to approach and destroy. From the rear the Achaeans hit us with arrows and stones, while in the front line our men faced their best warriors. We began to get scattered, lost. Polydamas, again, hurried to Hector; he was furious. "Hector! Will you listen to me? Just because you are the strongest, you think you are also the wisest, and you won't listen to others? Listen to me! The battle surrounds us like a crown of fire, and don't you see that the Trojans are in disarray? They don't know whether to go back to the wall or to go forward. We have to stop and make a plan or risk getting to the ships with only a few men, and I can't forget that Achilles is still there, waiting for us, hungry for war." He was right, and Hector knew it. He turned back, then, to gather his best warriors, to assemble the army again, and then he realized that many of us hadn't made it, had been struck down at the wall— Deiphobus, Helenus, Otryoneus, he looked for them but couldn't find them. He found Paris and railed against him, as if it were his fault that the others were gone. "They are dead, Hector," cried Paris. "Dead or wounded. We stayed to fight. Stop looking for the dead and lead us, those you have, into battle, to the ships. All our strength is with you, and will follow you." And as with Polydamas, so with Paris, Hector listened to him and again launched the attack, putting himself at the head and leading us with him.

AJAX

I saw him coming, protected by his shield, at the forefront of his men, with the shining helmet quivering over his temples. Then I almost started running toward him. "Come on, madman, let's go!" I shouted. "You want our ships, right? But we have arms with which to defend them, and with these arms we will annihilate you and your city. Start praying, Hector, because soon you'll need the swiftest horses in order to flee and save your life!"

SARPEDON

"What do you mean, Ajax," cried Hector. "You're just a lying show-off. This is the day of your ruin, believe me. You, too, will die, along with all the others. Come and challenge my spear. It can't wait to bite your white skin and leave you on the plain of Troy as a meal for dogs and birds!" And without delay he hurled his spear at Ajax.

AJAX

He hit me right in the chest, but I wasn't destined to die there. The bronze tip stopped just where the two thick straps of leather and silver meet, one for the shield, one for the sword— it stuck right there. So I bent over, took a sharp stone from the ground, and before Hector could hide among his men I threw it at him with all my might.

SARPEDON

The stone whirled through the air like a top, passed over the shield, and hit him hard, right below the neck. We saw him topple to the ground, like an oak struck by a thunderbolt.

AJAX

A cry went up, a great cry, and it was the cry of all the Achaeans, who rushed at him to carry him off, to tear him to pieces.

SARPEDON

But no one could touch him. We were all there to shelter him—Polydamas, Agenor, Glaucus, and a thousand others who with their shields made an insuperable barrier around him. Finally I took him in my arms and carried him out of the fray. I hurried back to the wall and then I crossed the trench, and didn't stop until I reached his chariot. We loaded him on it and then away, at a gallop, back to the plain. Only when we reached the river did we stop. Hector moaned, weakened. We laid him on the ground and poured water over his head. He opened his eyes, struggled to his knees, and vomited black blood; then he fell to the ground again, backward, and a dark shadow descended over his eyes.

AJAX

When I saw that they had taken him away, I knew it was the moment to attack. I went first, leading all behind me. It was a savage fight. Not so loud are the waves of the sea crashing against the cliffs when the north wind blows violently. Not so strong is the roar of a fire when it blazes up in the mountain valleys and consumes the forest, not so loud does the wind wail when it rages among the tall branches of the oaks—not so loud as the cry that exploded when Achaeans and Trojans charged. And first I killed Satnius, the son of Enops, goring him in the side; Polydamas killed Prothoënor, piercing him through the shoulder. I killed Archelochus with a blow that cut off his head; Acamas killed Promachus, and, to avenge Promachus, Peneleos assaulted Ilioneus, striking him under the eyebrow with his spear, so that the eye fell out and the point pierced the skull and emerged from the neck. Peneleos drew his sword and cut off the head, and then he raised his spear, with the head still attached to it, and waved it in the air, shouting, "Trojans, tell the parents of Ilioneus from me that they can begin to weep for him, because they will never again see the body of their beloved son!" It was something that terrified the Trojans. We saw them scatter, seeking an escape.

They felt the abyss of death opening before them. And suddenly they all began to run, and, fleeing, they abandoned the ships and reached the wall, but they didn't stop there, they went on running and crossed the trench, and only when they were on the other side, next to their chariots, did they stop, pale with fear.

SARPEDON

Frightened like deer pursued into the depths of the forest by hunters: with their loud bellowing, they wake a thick-maned lion, who springs from the obscurity of the woods and freezes every heart.

HECTOR

They thought I was dead. Suddenly they saw me before them, like a spirit escaped from the beyond, like a nightmare that wouldn't leave them in peace, like a lion that had sunk its teeth into their flesh and wouldn't let go. They fled, most of them, in retreat toward the ships. Only the bravest remained: Ajax, Idomeneus, Teucer, Meriones, Meges. With long strides I marched against them, leading the whole army behind me. One after another they fell under our attack. Stichius and Arcesilaus killed by me. Medon and Iasus killed by Aeneas. Mecisteus killed by Polydamas, Echius killed by Polites, Clonius killed by Agenor. Deiochus killed by Paris, struck in the back. While we stripped the bodies, they ran in every direction. Even the best, all of them. They retreated to the wall, but still fear gripped them, and they abandoned that, too, withdrawing toward the ships.

I shouted to my soldiers to leave the bodies and the

weapons and everything and jump in their chariots and launch into pursuit. The way was open; we could get to the ships without even fighting. Then I mounted my chariot and urged the horses to a gallop. We reached the trench, we crossed it, we headed for the wall, and everywhere overran it, and it crumbled like a sand castle under our assault. *I was at the very front and finally I saw, there, before me, the ships. The first black hulls, propped up on the land, and then, as far as the eye could see, ships, ships, ships down to the beach and the sea, thousands of masts and keels, prows pointing toward the sky as far as you could see. The ships. No one can understand what that war was for us Trojans without imagining the day we saw them arrive. There were more than a thousand, on that stretch of the sea that had been in our view since we were children, but we had never seen it touched by something that was not friendly, and small, and rare. Now it was obscured to the horizon by monsters come from far away to annihilate us. I understand what kind of war it was when I think back to that day, and see myself, my brothers—all the young men of Troy—outfitted in our glorious armor, as we came out of the city, marched across the plain, and, reaching the sea, tried to stop that terrifying fleet, by throwing stones. The stones on the beach. We threw them, do you understand? A thousand ships, and us with our stones.*

Nine years later, I again have those ships before me. But they are imprisoned on land, and surrounded by terrified men who with arms raised pray to heaven not to die. Is it surprising if I forgot my wound, the blow from Ajax, weariness, and fear? I unleashed my army, and it became for those ships a stormy sea, a swelling wave, and sparkling surf.

We scaled the keels, torches in hand, to set fire to the

ships. But the Achaeans made a strong defense. There was
Ajax again, urging them on, directing them. He was on a ship,
at the stern, and he was killing anyone who could get up or
even get near. I headed straight for him and, when I was close
enough, aimed and hurled my spear. The bronze tip flew high
but missed the target and struck Lycophron, one of his men. I
saw Ajax shudder, then glance at Teucer, without a pause in
the fighting. Teucer was the best archer among the Achaeans.
As if Ajax had given him an order, he took an arrow from the
quiver, stretched the bowstring, and aimed straight at me.
Instinctively I raised my shield, but what I saw was the bowstring break, and the arrow fall to earth, and Teucer, terrified,
freeze. Truly it seemed a sign from the gods. Auspicious for me
and unlucky for the Achaeans. I looked around. They had
made a shield for the ships, fighting close beside one another:
they were a wall of bronze that kept us back. I searched for a
weak point, where I could break through, but couldn't find
one. And so I went where I saw the finest armor and attacked
there, like a lion who attacks a flock that no shepherd can
save. They looked at me with terror. I was foaming with rage,
my temples were pounding under the shining helmet: they
looked at me and fled, the wall of bronze opened. I saw them
run toward the tents for a last stand, and I looked up and saw
the ships, just above me, closer than I had ever seen them.
Only Ajax remained, with a few men, jumping from one ship
to the next, waving a pike, and his voice rose to the sky as with
a terrible cry he called to the Achaeans to fight. I chose a ship
with a blue prow. I attacked from the stern, climbing up to the
deck. The Achaeans pressed around me. It was no longer the
moment for spears or arrows. We fought hand to hand, a
battle of swords, daggers, sharpened axes. I saw the blood run

in rivers down from the ship, down to the black earth. That was the battle I had always wished for: not in the open plain, not at the walls of Troy, but on the ships, the hated ships.

"Achaeans, soldiers, where did you leave your courage?" It was the voice of Ajax. There on the deck he fought and shouted. "Why are you fleeing? Do you think there is some-place behind you where you can take refuge? The sea is behind you; this is where we'll be saved!" I saw him just above me. He was covered with sweat, panting. He could hardly breathe, and weariness weighed down his arms. I raised my sword and with a sharp blow broke his spear, just below the tip; he stood there with the shaft, of ash, truncated, in his hand. In all that din I could hear the sound of the bronze tip as it fell to the wood of the deck. And Ajax understood—that it was my day, and that the gods were with me. He retreated, finally, he did it, he retreated. And I went up onto that ship. And I set fire to it.

It's amid those flames that you should remember me. Hector, the defeated, you should remember him standing on the stern of that ship, surrounded by fire. Hector, the dead man dragged by Achilles three times around the walls of his city, you should remember him alive, and victorious, and shining in his bronze and silver armor. I learned from a queen the words that are left to me now and that I would like to repeat to you: Remember me, remember me, and forget my fate.

PHOENIX

They were so young that to them I was an old man. A teacher, maybe a father. To see them die without being able to do anything, this was my war. As for the rest, who remembers it anymore?

What I remember is Patroclus rushing into Achilles' tent, weeping. It was that day of fierce battle, and defeat. He made an impression, Patroclus, in tears like that. He wept the way a little girl weeps as she clutches her mother's robe and asks to be picked up in her arms; and even when the mother's arms pick her up, she can't stop looking at her, looking at her and crying. He was a hero, and he seemed a little child, a baby. "What's the matter?" Achilles asked him. "Have you heard news of someone dying in our homeland? Maybe your father has died, or mine? Or do you weep for the Achaeans, who because of their arrogance are dying beside the black ships?" He would not give up his anger, do you understand? But that day Patroclus, amid his tears, asked him to listen, without rage, without anger, without malice. Only to listen.

"Today, Achilles, great suffering has come upon the Achaeans. Those who were the bravest and the strongest lie wounded on the ships. Diomedes, Odysseus, Agamemnon: the healers are struggling, trying to soothe their wounds with every sort of drug. And you, mighty warrior, sit here, closed up in your anger. So I want you to listen to mine, Achilles, my anger: my rage. You don't want to fight. I do. Send me into battle with your Myrmidon warriors. Give me your armor. Let me put it on. The Trojans will take me for you, and they will flee. Give me your armor and we'll drive them back, back to the walls of Troy." He spoke in the voice of a suppliant: he couldn't know that he was asking to die.

Achilles listened to him. It was clear that the words disturbed him. Finally he spoke, and what he said changed the war. "A tremendous sorrow strikes the heart when a powerful king, thanks to his power, steals from a man what is due him. And this is the sorrow I feel, that Agamemnon has inflicted on me. But it's true, what's been done can't be changed. And maybe no heart can cultivate an unyielding anger forever. I said I wouldn't move until I heard the din of battle resounding near my black ship. That moment has arrived. Take my armor, Patroclus, take my men. Go into battle and keep disaster from the ships. Drive the Trojans back before they take from us the hope of a sweet return. But listen carefully and do what I tell you, if you really want to restore my honor and glory to me: once you've driven the enemy back from the ships, stop— don't pursue the Trojans onto the plain. Stop fighting and come back. Don't deprive me of my share of honor and glory. Don't get excited by the tumult of battle and the cries that will urge you on to fight and kill all the way to the walls of Troy.

Leave that to the others and return, Patroclus. Come back here."

Then he rose, banishing all his sadness, and in a strong voice said, "Now hurry, put on the armor. Already I see the flames of deathly fire burning near my ship. Hurry up, I will assemble the men."

Who was I to stop them? Can a teacher, a father, stop destiny? Patroclus clothed himself in gleaming bronze. He put on the beautiful greaves with silver fastenings at the ankles. On his chest he placed Achilles' breastplate: it sparkled like a star. He slung over his shoulders the sword adorned with silver and then the big, heavy shield. On his proud head he placed the well-made helmet: the horsehair crest fluttered fearfully. Finally he chose two spears. But he didn't take the one belonging to Achilles. Only Achilles could lift it, the ash spear Cheiron had given his father that he might bring death to heroes.

When he came out of the tent, the Myrmidons gathered close around him, ready for battle. They were like ravenous wolves whose spirits are bold. Fifty ships had brought Achilles to Troy. Five battalions of warriors, commanded by five heroes. Menesthius, Eudorus, Pisander, Alcimedon. The fifth was me. Phoenix, the old man. Achilles spoke to all of us, sternly. "Myrmidons, you have accused me of having a heart of stone and of keeping you on the ships, far from the battle, only to nurse my anger. Well, now you have the war you longed for. Fight with all the courage you possess." At the echo of his voice, the ranks of fighters closed in, and, like stones in a wall, the men pressed together. Shield to shield, helmet to helmet, man to man, they were so tightly arrayed that at every movement the plumes in the crests of the shining helmets touched. At the head of them all Patroclus: in the chariot to which Automedon had yoked Xanthus and Balius, the two immortal stallions, swift as the wind, and Pedasus, a mortal horse and handsome.

Achilles went into his tent and lifted the cover of a splendid chest, all inlaid, that his mother had had brought onto the ship so that he could take it with him: it was full of tunics, mantles, and heavy coverings. There was also a precious cup that only Achilles could use, and used to drink only in homage to Zeus, and to no other god. He took it, purified it with sulfur, then washed it in clear water, washed his hands, and finally poured into it sparkling wine. Then he came out, and before us all drank the wine and, gazing up to heaven, prayed to almighty Zeus that Patroclus would fight, and win, and return. And all of us together with him.

We fell on the Trojans suddenly, like a furious swarm of wasps. The black hulls of the ships resounded with our cries. Patroclus, in the forefront, magnificent in the armor of Achilles, gave a shout. And the Trojans saw him, dazzling, in the chariot, beside Automedon. Achilles, they thought. And suddenly confusion reigned in their army, and despair consumed their souls. The abyss of death opened under their feet as they tried to escape. The first spear to fly was that of Patroclus, hurled straight into the heart of the tumult: it struck Pyraechmes, the leader of the Paeonians, hit him in the right shoulder, and he fell with a cry; gripped by fear, the Paeonians vanished, abandoning the ship they had boarded and had already half burned.

Patroclus put out the fire and rushed toward the other ships. The Trojans didn't give up. They retreated, but they were unwilling to leave the ships. The contest was brutal, and hard. One after another all our heroes had to fight, to overcome the enemy; one after another the Trojans fell, until it was too much, even for them, and they began to scatter and flee, like sheep pursued by a pack of savage wolves. The hooves of the galloping horses raised a cloud of dust into the sky. They fled in a tumultuous uproar, covering every path to the horizon. And where their flight was thickest, Patroclus attacked, shouting and killing, and many men fell under his hands, many chariots overturned with a crash.

But the truth is that he wanted Hector: in his heart, secretly, he was looking for Hector, for his own honor and his own glory. And at a certain point he saw him among the Trojans, who, fleeing, were trying to get back across the trench, he saw him and pursued him. Around him everywhere were warriors in flight: the trench hindered their course, making everything difficult. The poles of the Trojans' chariots broke and the horses galloped away, like rivers in flood, but Hector—he had the ability of great warriors, and he made his way through the battle with an ear for the whiz of spears and the whistle of arrows, he knew where to go, how to move, he knew when to stay with his companions and when to abandon them, he knew how to hide and how to be seen. His horses, swift as the wind, bore him away, and Patroclus turned then and began to drive the Trojans back toward the ships, cutting off their flight and pushing them again toward the ships. It was there that he wanted to close in and annihilate them.

He struck Pronous in the breast where the shield had left it unprotected. He saw Thestor huddled in his chariot, as if dazed, and gored him in the jaw, sending the spear's bronze tip through his skull. Patroclus raised the spear as if he had caught a fish, lifting the body of Thestor up over the edge of the chariot, openmouthed—and then with a rock he struck Erylaus between the eyes. Inside the helmet his head split in two. The hero fell to the ground, and upon him life-destroying death descended, and descended also upon Erymas, Amphoterus, Epaltes, Tlepolemus, Echius, Pyris, Ipheus, Euippus, Polymelus, all by the hand of Patroclus.

"Shame on you!" It was the voice of Sarpedon, the son of Zeus and leader of the Lycians. "Shame to flee before this man! I will challenge him. I want to know who he is." He got out of his chariot and Patroclus saw him, and he, too, got out. They stood facing each other like two vultures who fight on a high cliff, with curved beaks and sharp claws. Slowly they walked toward each other. Sarpedon's spear flew high over Patroclus's left shoulder, but Patroclus struck Sarpedon in the chest, just where the heart is. He fell like a tall oak brought down by men's axes to become the keel of a ship. He lay beside his chariot, groaning, his hands scratching at the bloody dirt. He was dying like an animal. With the life that remained he called on his friend Glaucus, entreating him, "Glaucus, don't let them strip me of my armor. Rally the Lycian fighters, come and defend me. You will be dishonored forever if you allow Patroclus to carry off my armor, Glaucus!"

Patroclus approached, placed his foot on his chest, and pulled out the spear, taking with it the guts and the heart. Thus, in a single gesture, he carried off from that body the bronze point and life itself. Meanwhile, Glaucus, mad with grief, rushed from place to place, calling together all the Lycian chiefs and Trojan heroes. "Sarpedon is dead, Patroclus has killed him. Come and defend his armor!" And they ran to him, stricken by the death of that man who was one of the bravest and most beloved defenders of Troy. They ran and closed their ranks around the body, Hector in the lead, to defend it. Patroclus saw them coming and he assembled us, then, and arrayed us opposite, saying that if we were truly the bravest of all, this was the moment to show it. There was the body of Sarpedon in the middle, Trojans and Lycians on one side, we Myrmidons on the other. And it was a battle, for that body and that armor.

At first the Trojans overwhelmed us. But when Patroclus saw his friends around him giving way under the assault, he rushed into the front line and, like a hawk that puts crows and starlings to flight, fell on the enemy, driving them back. From the earth rose a din of bronze, of leather, of the thick hides of oxen, under the blows of swords and double-pointed spears. No man, however acute, would by now have been able to recognize the body of Sarpedon, because from head to foot it was covered with arrows and dust and blood. We continued to fight over that corpse without respite, like flies in a barn buzzing ceaselessly around the pails of white milk. And it went on like that until Hector did something surprising. Maybe fear had overwhelmed him; I don't know. We saw him jump in his chariot, and, turning his back, he fled, shouting to his men to follow. And, indeed, they followed, abandoning Sarpedon's body and the battlefield.

There was something I didn't understand. They ran toward their city. A few hours earlier they had been on our ships setting fire to our hopes, and now they were fleeing toward their city. We should have let them go. That was what Achilles had said. Drive them from the ships but then stop, come back. We should have let them go. But Patroclus couldn't stop. The courage in his heart was great, and the fate of death that awaited him clear.

He threw himself into pursuit and drew us all along with him. He never stopped killing as he rushed toward the walls of Troy. Adrastus, Autonous, Echeclus, Perimus all fell under his assault, and then Epistor, Melanippus, Elasus, Mulius,

Pylartes, and when he reached the Scaean gates he charged the tower—once, and then a second time, and yet again, always repulsed by the Trojans' shining shields, and a fourth time—before giving up. I looked around then to find Hector. He seemed undecided whether to draw the army back inside the walls or stay and fight. Now I know there was no doubt in his mind, but only the instinct of the great warrior. I saw him gesture to Cebriones, his driver. Then his chariot hurtled into the heart of the battle. I saw Hector upright in the chariot. Passing among the soldiers without even taking the trouble to kill, he simply cut through the throng and headed straight for Patroclus. That was where he wanted to go.

Patroclus understood and jumped down from his chariot. He bent down and picked up a sharp white rock off the ground. And when Hector's chariot was in range he hurled it with all his strength. The rock struck Cebriones, the driver, who was holding the reins in his hands. It struck him in the forehead, the bone split, his eyes fell out on the ground, in the dust, and he, too, fell. "What agility," Patroclus began to mock him. "You know what an expert fisherman you would be, Cebriones, if only you could dive into water as skillfully as you spring from a chariot. Who ever said there are no good swimmers among the Trojans?" He laughed—and found himself facing Hector.

As two famished lions in the mountains fight furiously over a dead deer, so the two began to fight for the body of Cebriones. Hector had taken the dead man by the head and wouldn't let go. Patroclus had grabbed him by the feet and tried to drag him away. Around them a savage struggle arose, Trojans against Achaeans, over the corpse.

We fought for hours over that man who by now was in the dust, heedless of chariots and horses and all that had been his life. When, in the end, we managed to drive the Trojans back, some of us seized the body and dragged it far from the fray to strip it. But Patroclus remained in the heart of the fight. It was no longer possible to stop him. Three times he hurled himself on the Trojans with a terrible cry, and killed nine men. But when he launched himself the fourth time, like a god, then, Patroclus, suddenly we all saw the end of your life appear. It was Euphorbus, and he struck you from behind, in the back. He arrived in his chariot, advancing through the fray. There was dust everywhere, an enormous cloud of dust. You didn't see him coming. He appeared as if out of nowhere, suddenly, behind you, and you couldn't see him. I saw him. From close up he thrust the spear in your back . . . *Do you remember Euphorbus, Patroclus, do you remember that we saw him in battle and remarked on his beauty; his hair hung long over his shoulders, and wasn't he the most beautiful of all? . . .* He struck you in the back and then, immediately, dashed off to hide among his men, in fear of what he had just done.

Patroclus was motionless, stunned. His eyes rolled upward. His legs still supported that handsome body but no longer felt it. I remember his head lolling forward after the blow, and the helmet falling in the dust. That helmet, never would I have thought to see it grimed with dust and blood, on the ground. The helmet that had covered the head and beautiful face of godlike Achilles, I saw it rolling on the ground amid the horses' hooves, in the dust and the blood.

Patroclus took a few steps, searched for something that might hide or save him. He didn't want to die. Around him everything had come to a halt. *Certain deaths are rituals, but you can't understand. No one stopped Hector when he approached. This you can't understand.* Into the fray he went, with none of us able to stop him. He came within a step and then thrust the spear through his belly. And Patroclus fell to the ground. We all saw him, this time, crumple to the ground, and then Hector, leaning over him, looking him in the eyes and speaking to him in that icy silence.

"Patroclus, you thought you would come here and destroy my city, right? You imagined returning home with a ship full of Trojan woman and Trojan treasure. Now you know that Troy is defended by brave men, and the bravest is called Hector. You are nothing now. You are food for the vultures. He won't be much help to you, your friend Achilles, no matter how brave he is. It's he, right, who sent you here. It's he who told you, 'Don't come back, Patroclus, until you have ripped open Hector's chest and bloodied his tunic.' And you, you fool, listened to him."

Patroclus was dying, but still he found the strength to speak. "You can boast now, Hector, because you have vanquished me. But the truth is that to die was my destiny. The gods killed me, and among men Euphorbus was first. You, who are now ending my life, are only the third, Hector. You are only the last of those who killed me. And now listen to me, and don't forget what I have to tell you. You are a dead man who is walking, Hector. Nothing can save you from your atrocious fate. The little life you have left—Achilles will come and tear it away from you."

Then the veil of death enveloped him. His soul flew away and went to Hades, mourning lost strength, lost youth.

Hector placed his foot on Patroclus's chest and drew the bronze spear out of the wound. The body rose up and then, lacerated, fell back in the dust. Hector stood there looking at it. He said something in a low voice. Then, as if seized by a fury, he was about to attack Automedon and would have killed him, but the swift horses carried him away, the horses that the gods gave to Achilles carried him away from Hector's grasp, from his rage and from death.

I died two years later, during the voyage on which I was seeking to return home from Troy. It was Neoptolemus who burned my body. He was the son of Achilles. Now my bones lie in a land whose name I don't even know. Maybe it's right that it ended like that, since I would never have been able truly to return from that war, from that bloodshed, and from the death of two boys I couldn't save.

ANTILOCHUS

The first to realize that Patroclus was dead was Menelaus. He rushed to the spot and stood beside the body with his spear and his shield thrust forward, ready to kill anyone who approached. Euphorbus arrived, the one who had struck Patroclus first: he wanted to get his trophy. But Menelaus shouted at him, "Stay away, if you don't want to die! You know what happened to your brother when he challenged me. He didn't go home on his own two legs, to bring joy to his wife and his parents. I'll kill you, too, if you don't get away." Euphorbus was the most beautiful of the Trojans. He had shining curls wound around his head and fastened with pins of gold and silver. He told Menelaus that he would avenge his brother, and hurled the spear at him. The bronze tip broke on the shield, and Menelaus leaped on him and plunged the spear into his throat, driving it in with the full weight of his arm. The point passed through his graceful neck, and his hair was bathed in blood. He fell to the ground like an olive tree, young, beautiful, strong, covered with white blossoms, suddenly shattered by a bolt of lightning in a storm.

Menelaus was bending down to strip him of his armor when he realized that Hector was rushing at him, with a terrible cry. Frightened, he abandoned the body of Patroclus and began to retreat, looking all around for someone to help him. He saw Ajax and shouted, "Patroclus is dead, Ajax, and Hector is taking his armor. Come, we have to defend him." Ajax turned and his heart was moved. He rushed to his aid. They returned to Patroclus and saw that Hector had taken the glorious armor and now had drawn his sword to cut off the head and abandon the body there, a meal for the dogs. Ajax set on him with such ferocity that Hector gave up his prey and withdrew among his men. Ajax bent over the body of Patroclus and covered it with his immense towering shield: he stood there as a lion stands beside its cubs when it catches the scent of the hunters.

The Trojans realized that Hector had run from Ajax, and they looked at him in bewilderment. I remember that I heard Glaucus shouting, "You're a coward, Hector, you didn't challenge Ajax because he's stronger than you, and now you have left him the body of Patroclus, which would have been a precious prize for us!" Then Hector did something that no one will forget. He ran to join his companions who were carrying Patroclus's armor into the city, a trophy. He stopped them, took off his own armor, and put on the immortal armor that Achilles had given to his friend to go into battle. He put it on and it became his, the immortal armor of Achilles. His body in that armor, he seemed born for that armor, and suddenly he shone with strength and vigor. Brilliant he strode before all his men in the gleaming armor that for years they had looked at with terror, and now it was he who showed it off before their eyes.

They looked in amazement, Glaucus, Medon, Thersilochus, Asteropaeus. They watched him pass, rapt—Deisenor, Hippothous, Phorcys, Chromius, Ennomus—and to them Hector cried, "Fight alongside me, allies of a thousand tribes. I tell you that whoever can bring the body of Patroclus among the Trojans, overpowering Ajax, will share it with me and the glory will be equal for me and for him." And in a fury they charged toward the Achaeans.

Ajax saw them coming and realized that neither he nor Menelaus could stop them. So he called for help, and first Idomeneus, then Meriones and Oilean Ajax and other brave men heard him and rushed to his side. The Trojans charged in a mass, all behind Hector. Around Ajax the Achaeans were arrayed with a single heart, protected by the bronze shields. The first wave of Trojans pushed them back, forcing them to abandon the body. But Ajax led his men to the attack again, until they managed to seize it from the hands of the Trojans. It was a tremendous struggle, a fearful contest. Toil and sweat grimed the legs and knees, the feet and hands and eyes of those who were fighting for the body. From every direction men grabbed the body of Patroclus and pulled, and it was like the skin of an animal when it is stretched for drying. Patroclus . . .

Nor did Achilles yet know that his beloved friend was dead. His tent was far away, near the black ships, and Patroclus had gone to die at the walls of Troy. He couldn't know. I imagined him there, in his tent, still thinking that soon Patroclus would return, after driving the Trojans away, and he would give back the armor, and they would feast together, and . . . and while he was thinking these things, at that very moment Patroclus was already a corpse, contested on every side, and around him men were killing one another, and sharp spears flashed, and bronze shields clashed in the din. *This we*

*should learn about suffering: it is the child of Zeus. And Zeus
is the child of Cronus.*

And the story of Xanthus and Balius? On the subject of
suffering . . . they were Achilles' immortal steeds, and had carried Patroclus into battle. Well, when Patroclus fell, Automedon led them far from the fray, thinking to get them to safety
by galloping to the ships. But when they reached the middle of
the plain they stopped, suddenly, immobilized, because their
hearts were broken by grief at the death of Patroclus. Automedon tried to make them go, with the whip and with gentle
entreaties, but they wouldn't return to the ships. They stood
motionless, like a marble monument on a man's tomb, with
their muzzles brushing the earth, and they wept, says the legend, their eyes wept burning tears. They were not born to suffer old age or death, they were immortal. But they had run
beside man, and from him they had learned grief: because
there is nothing on the face of the earth, nothing that breathes
or walks, nothing so unhappy as man. Finally, abruptly, the
two horses launched into a gallop, but in the direction of the
fighting. Automedon tried to stop them, but there was nothing
to do. They headed for the thick of it, as they would have done
in any battle, you see? But Automedon, in the chariot, was
alone, he had to hold the reins. He couldn't take up his
weapons, and so he could kill no one. They carried him among
the warriors and into the tumult, but the truth is that he
couldn't fight, the truth is that it seemed a mad chariot, which
passed through the battle like a wind without striking a blow,
absurd and marvelous.

Then the Achaeans realized that they were about to lose
that battle. Some, like Idomeneus, abandoned the field, giving
up. The others thought of returning to the ships, but without
ceasing to fight, and trying to carry off the body of Patroclus.

Someone said, too, that Achilles had to be told what had happened, and all agreed, except that they didn't know whom to send. They needed the fighters there, and then maybe no one wanted to be the one to bring Achilles the news of Patroclus's death. Finally they chose a boy whom Achilles was fond of and who, at that moment, was fighting far from the body of Patroclus. And I was that boy.

My name is Antilochus. I am one of Nestor's sons. When my father left for the war in Troy I was too young to go with him. So I stayed home. But five years later, without saying anything to my father, I took a ship and landed on the beach at Troy. I introduced myself to Achilles and I told him the truth, that I had run away to fight beside him. My father will kill me, I said. Achilles admired my courage and my beauty. And so it was. I became one of them, and, with a boy's folly, I fought beside them in that war, until the day when, in the middle of the fighting, I saw Menelaus hurrying toward me, in fact he was searching for me, and when he got close he looked me in the eye and said, "Patroclus is dead, Antilochus. I would never have wanted to bring you such news, but the truth is that Patroclus is dead, killed by the Trojans." I couldn't say anything, only I began to cry, right there, in the middle of the battle. I heard the voice of Menelaus shouting at me, "You must run to the ships, to Achilles, and tell him that Patroclus is dead, and that he has to do something, because we're trying to carry his body to safety, but the Trojans are on us and are too strong for us. Go, hurry."

And I went. I took off my armor so that I would be lighter and ran across the plain, weeping all the way. When I reached the ships, I found Achilles standing and scanning the horizon, trying to see what was happening in the battle. I stopped in front of him. I don't know where I looked when I began to speak: "Achilles, son of brave Peleus, something happened that should never have happened, and I have to bring you the news. Patroclus is dead, and the Achaeans are fighting for his naked body, because Hector has taken his armor."

A black cloud of grief enveloped the hero. He fell to the ground and with both hands began clawing at the dirt and pouring it on his head and his handsome face. From the tents the women made slaves by war came running and around him began wailing with grief, falling to their knees and beating their breasts. Achilles sobbed. I leaned over him and held his hands tight in mine, because I didn't want him to kill himself with those hands and a sharp blade. He gave a tremendous cry and called on his mother.

"Mother! I asked for sorrow to come upon the Achaeans, to make them pay for their insult to me, but how can I be happy now? Now I have lost forever the one whom I honored above all my companions and whom I loved like myself! He died far from his homeland, and I wasn't there to protect him. I was sitting in my tent, you see? I was sitting beside my ship, like a useless weight on the earth. While he was dying and so many were dying under Hector's assault, I was here, I who am the best of the Achaeans in battle . . . Oh, if only anger would vanish forever from men's hearts, which can make even the wisest into fools, slipping into their souls with the sweetness of honey, then rising like smoke into their minds. I must forget my bitterness. I must go away from here and find the man who killed my beloved companion. Then I, too, will die, I know, Mother, but first with my spear I want to crush the life of that man, and around me sow so much death that the women of Troy will long for the days when this war was fought without me." These things he said, weeping, but still he lay there, in the dust.

Then I said to him, "Rise, Achilles, the Achaeans need you now. They are trying to defend the body of Patroclus from the Trojans, but the fight is brutal and many are dying. Hector is in a fury. He wants that corpse, he wants to cut off the head to stick on a pole and raise it aloft as a trophy. Don't stay here, Achilles. What sort of dishonor will it be if you let Patroclus end as food for Trojan dogs?"

Achilles looked at me. "How can I return to battle?" he said. "My armor is in the hands of the Trojans, and I can't fight with armor that isn't worthy of me. What hero would? How can I?"

Then I said, "I know, your armor is in the hands of Hector, but even so, without your armor, rise up and let the Trojans see you. They'll be terrified, and our men will at least be able to catch their breath."

And so he rose. He walked toward the edge of the trench, toward the battle. He could see our men running back, carrying high in their arms the body of Patroclus, and Hector was pursuing them with his men, following without pity. It was like taking carrion away from a starving lion. They tried to keep him away, the two Ajaxes, and every time he came back, like a fire that suddenly flares up to attack a city. Achilles stopped on the higher edge of the trench. He had no armor on now, but he shone like a flame, like a golden cloud. He gazed at the battle and let out a loud cry, like the peal of a trumpet. The Trojans were petrified. The horses with their beautiful manes reared up, scenting the odor of death. Three times Achilles cried out, and three times terror descended into the hearts of the Trojans. We saw them turn their chariots and flee, leaving the battle, consumed by anguish.

When our men placed the body of Patroclus on a litter, in

safety, Achilles approached. He placed his hands on the chest of his beloved friend, gently, those hands that were used to killing. He placed them on his chest and began to sob without respite, like a lion whose cubs have been stolen by hunters out of the depths of the forest.

AGAMEMNON

They wept over the body all night. They had washed away the blood and dust and had anointed the wounds with the richest unguent. So that he would not lose his beauty, they had dripped nectar and ambrosia in his nostrils. Then they had placed the body on the funeral bed, wrapped in soft linen, and covered by a white robe. *Patroclus: he was only a boy. I'm not even sure he was a hero. Now they had made him a god.*

Dawn rose over their laments, *and the day came that I would remember forever as the day of my end.* They brought Achilles armor that the most skilled Achaean artisans had made for him that night, working with divine inspiration. They placed it at his feet. He had embraced the body of Patroclus and was sobbing. He turned to look at the armor, and his eyes glittered with a sinister light. It was armor such as no one had ever seen or worn. It seemed made by a god for a god. *It was a temptation that Achilles never could have resisted.*

So finally he rose and left the body and, shouting, and

striding among the ships, called the men to assemble. I realized
that our war would be decided then and there when I saw even
the ships' pilots coming, and the kitchen stewards, men who
never joined the assemblies. But that day they, too, were present, drawing close around the heroes and princes to know
their fate. I waited until they were seated. I waited until Ajax
arrived, until Odysseus took his place, in the first row. They
were limping because of their wounds. Then, last of all, I
entered the assembly.

Achilles stood up. Everyone was silent. "Agamemnon," he
said, "it wasn't a good idea to quarrel, you and I, over a girl. If
only she had died right away, as soon as she came to my ship,
so many Achaeans wouldn't have bitten the infinite earth
while I sat far away, a prisoner of my rage. What's done is
done: it's time to master our hearts and forget the past. Today
I put aside my anger and return to the battle. You assemble the
Achaeans and urge them to fight with me, so that the Trojans
will never again sleep beside our ships."

On every side the men rejoiced. In all that clamor I began
to speak. I remained seated in my place and asked them to be
silent. I, the king of kings, had to ask for silence. Then I said,
"Many have reproached me because I took from Achilles his
prize of honor that day. And now I know I was wrong. But
even the gods make mistakes! Folly has light feet and she
doesn't touch the ground, but she walks in the heads of men,
leading them to ruin: she seizes them, one by one, when it
most pleases her. She seized me that day, took possession of
my senses. Now I want to compensate for that mistake by
offering you infinite gifts, Achilles."

He listened to me. Then he said that he would accept my
gifts, but not that day. That day it was urgent to go into battle
without wasting any more time, because a great undertaking

awaited him. He was so madly eager for war that he was incapable of waiting even an hour.

Then Odysseus rose. "Achilles," he said, "you can't take an army into battle without first feeding it. All day the men will have to fight, until sunset, and only he who has eaten and drunk can sustain the fight with a firm heart and strong limbs. Listen to me: send the men to the ships to prepare a meal. And meanwhile we'll have the gifts from Agamemnon brought here, to the assembly, so that we may all see and admire them. And then let Agamemnon solemnly swear before us that he did not unite with Briseis as men and women do. Your heart will be more serene when you go into battle. And you, Agamemnon, arrange a rich feast in your tent for Achilles, so that justice may be properly done. It's a worthy thing for a king to ask forgiveness if he has offended someone."

Thus he spoke. But Achilles wouldn't listen. "The earth is covered with the dead that Hector sowed behind him, and you want to eat? We'll eat at sunset. I want this army to fight famished. Patroclus lies dead and awaits his revenge: I tell you that neither food nor drink will pass my lips before I have had it. I don't care about gifts and feasts now. I want blood, and slaughter, and sorrow."

Thus he spoke. *But Odysseus was not the type to yield. Anyone else would have given in—I would have—but not he.* "Achilles, bravest of all the Achaeans, you are stronger than I am with the spear, certainly, but I am wiser than you, because I'm old and have seen many things. Accept my counsel. It will be a long battle, and a hard struggle awaits us before we win. It's fitting to weep over our dead: but must we do it with our stomachs? Isn't it also right to refresh ourselves when we're weary, getting strength from food and wine? Let us bury our dead with a firm heart, and weep from dawn until sunset. But then let's think of ourselves, so that we may return and eagerly pursue the enemy without respite, without pause, in our bronze armor. So I order that no one shall go into battle before eating and drinking. Then we'll attack the Trojans together and rouse the cruel battle again."

Thus he spoke, and they obeyed. Achilles, too, obeyed. Odysseus took some young men and went to my tent. He brought out, one by one, the gifts I had promised, tripods, horses, women, gold. And Briseis. He brought everything to the middle of the assembled crowd and then he looked at me. I rose. I was mad with pain from the wound in my arm, but I stood up. I, the king of kings, raised my arms to heaven and before them all I repeated these words: "I swear before Zeus and the Earth and the Sun and the Erinyes that I never touched this girl who is called Briseis, nor did I ever share my bed with her. In my tent she remained, and now I give her back untouched. May the gods inflict harsh punishments on me if this is not the truth."

I wasn't lying. I had taken that girl, but not her heart. I saw her weeping over the body of Patroclus and heard her speak as I had never before heard her. "Patroclus, you who were so dear to my heart! I left you living, and now I find you dead. There is no end to my misfortune. I saw my husband die, ravaged by Achilles' spear, and I saw all my brothers die beside the walls of my city. And when I grieved for them you comforted me and sweetly told me that you would take me to Phthia and that there Achilles would take me as his wife, and all together we would celebrate the wedding, joyfully. That sweetness I mourn today as I mourn you, Patroclus." And she embraced the body, sobbing, amid the laments of the other women.

Achilles waited for the army to take its meal. He wouldn't

touch food or wine. When the men began to stream out of the tents and the ships, ready for battle, he put on his new armor. The beautiful greaves with clasps of silver at the ankles; the breastplate over his chest; the sword slung over his shoulders; the helmet on his head, glittering like a star. And the spear, the famous spear that his father had given him, to bring death to heroes. Last of all he took the shield: it was huge and strong, it glowed like the moon. The entire cosmos was carved into it: the earth and the waters, men and stars, the living and the dead. *We fought with weapons in our hands: that man was going into battle holding the world.*

I saw him, radiant as the sun, get into his chariot and call to his immortal horses to carry him to revenge. He was angry with them because they hadn't been able to save Patroclus from death. So he shouted and insulted them. And the legend says that in response they lowered their muzzles and, pulling on the reins, answered with a human voice, and they said to him: We will run swift as the wind, Achilles, but swifter than us runs your fate, toward death.

THE RIVER

I had seen years of war, because a river does not run blindly among men. And for years I had heard their groans, because a river does not run deaf where men are dying. Always impassively I had carried to the sea the discharge of that ferocious conflict. But that day the blood was too much, and the savagery, and the hatred. On the day of Achilles' glory I rebelled, in horror. If you're not afraid of fables, listen to this one.

It was dawn, and the two immense armies were arrayed, facing each other, at the Achaeans' wall. I saw the bronze armor flash in the light of the early sun. There stood Achilles before his men in the new armor, imposing, godlike. And in the front line, at the head of the Trojans, Aeneas, the son of Anchises. He advanced, tossing his head in the heavy helmet and waving his bronze-tipped spear. Achilles expected no less. He bounded forth from the ranks of his men, planting himself right in front of Aeneas: he was foaming with rage like a wounded lion and like a wounded lion was hungry for revenge and for blood. He began to shout. "Aeneas, what do you have in mind—maybe you want to challenge me? Do you think that if you win, Priam will give you his crown? He has Hector, and so many other sons—you don't think he'll give his power to you? Go while you still have time. We've already met once, the two of us, and you remember how it went: you stayed only long enough to flee. Flee again, this time, right now: turn and run. And don't come back."

"Do you really think you can frighten me?" answered Aeneas. "I'm not a child, I'm a hero. There is noble blood and divine blood in my veins, as in yours. And I have no wish to stand here exchanging insults with you, as if we were gossipy old women quarreling in the street, rather than two heroes in the midst of combat and slaughter. Stop talking, Achilles, and fight."

He gripped the spear in his hand and hurled it. The bronze tip resounded against Achilles' enormous shining shield. It had been fashioned with immeasurable skill. Two layers of bronze on the outside, two layers of tin inside. And in the middle a layer of gold. Aeneas's spear pierced the bronze but not the gold.

Then Achilles raised his spear. Aeneas extended the arm that held the shield. The bronze tip flew swiftly through the air, tore the shield, passed over Aeneas's head by a hair, and stuck in the ground behind him. Aeneas stood petrified with fear. The throw had just missed him. Achilles drew his sword. With a terrible cry he rushed forward. Aeneas felt that he was lost. He picked up a large rock that was lying nearby. He raised it to defend himself. And I saw Achilles suddenly, as if blinded, lose his momentum, as if something had happened in his head, until he stopped, dazed, staring, as if searching for something he had lost. Aeneas didn't pause to think about it.

He turned and ran until he disappeared among the Trojans. So Achilles, when he came to himself, looked around and no longer saw him. There was the spear that had missed him by a hair sticking in the ground, but he wasn't there. "It's magic," Achilles murmured. "Aeneas must be dear to some god, to be able to disappear like that. But let him go to the dogs! He's not the one who concerns me. It's time to enter the battle." So he spoke, and attacked the Trojans.

First he killed Iphition, struck him in the head. His head split in two, the hero fell with a crash, and the wheels of the Achaean chariots rolled over him. Then he killed Demoleon, striking him in the temple. The bronze helmet couldn't withstand the blow and the point of the spear made pulp of his brains. Darkness descended over the hero's eyes. Then he killed Hippodamas as he was trying to flee, terrified. Hit in the back, he fell to the ground, gasping like an animal. The soul left the hero's body. Then he killed Polydorus, the youngest of Priam's sons, and the most beloved. Achilles struck him in the back; the spear went through his body and emerged from his chest. The hero fell to his knees with a cry, and a cloud enveloped him darkly.

When Hector saw his young brother on his knees, with his guts in his hands, he was filled with rage and forgot all caution. He knew that he shouldn't go out into the open, that he should wait for Achilles in the midst of the throng, where he was well protected by his companions. But when he saw his brother dying like that, he forgot everything and rushed forward toward Achilles, shouting.

Achilles saw him and in his eyes flashed a gleam of triumph. "Come on, Hector, come closer," he cried. "Approach your death!"

"You don't scare me, Achilles," he answered. "I know

you're stronger than I am, but my spear, like yours, can kill. And fate will decide who dies."

Then he hurled his weapon, but the bronze point hit the ground not far from Achilles. Achilles thought he had him in his power. With a tremendous cry he charged forward, brandishing his spear. But again his sight was clouded, and his mind wandered. Three times he charged forward, but as if blindly, as if he were enveloped in a thick fog. When he returned to himself, Hector was no longer there: he had disappeared amid the Trojans. Furious, Achilles attacked whoever came near. He killed Dryops, striking him in the neck. And Demuchus, hitting him first in the knee and then the belly. Laogonus he killed with the spear, and Dardanus with the sword. Tros, in terror, fell to his knees, asking for mercy. He was only a boy, young as Achilles. Achilles pierced his liver with a thrust of the sword; the liver spurted out, and black blood gushed from the hero's body. He killed Mulius with a blow to the ear; the bronze point went through his head and came out under the other ear. With his sword he killed Echeclus, ripping open his skull. With his spear he hit Deucalion's elbow, and then with the sword cut off his head. The marrow burst from his vertebrae; the hero's body fell to the ground. With his spear he gored Rhigmus in the stomach and killed his attendant Areithous with a blow to the back. He was like a fire that burns a vast forest, driven by a raging wind. The blood flowed over the black earth. And, eager for glory, his hands fouled with mud and death, he wouldn't stop.

Terrorized, the Trojans fled into the fields. And when they saw me, in the middle of the plain, like animals fleeing a conflagration they jumped into my waters in search of safety. Achilles reached the bank, laid his spear on the ground, and, unsheathing his sword, leaped in after them. He started killing whoever came within range. I heard moans and suffering everywhere, while my waters turned red with blood. I saw Achilles take twelve Trojan youths, one by one, and, instead of murdering them, carry them to the shore, to make them prisoners and sacrifice them before the body of Patroclus: one by one he dragged them out of the water, like startled fawns, to kill them beside the black ships. Then he turned to go back into the throng, to continue the slaughter. He was still on the shore when Lycaon appeared before him: he was a boy, and his father, Priam, had ransomed him from captivity. He had just returned to the battle. Now there he was, without armor, without weapons. He had thrown everything off so he could cross the river, and there he was, naked and afraid.

"What do my eyes see?" said Achilles. "I met you in battle once already and I took you alive, to sell you as a slave in Lemnos. And now I find you here again. Next, the Trojans I've sent to Hades will start reappearing. But this time you won't be back, Lycaon." He raised his spear and was about to strike him, but Lycaon dropped to his knees and the spear grazed his back and stuck in the ground.

"Have pity." Lycaon began to weep. "I've just returned to the battle and I meet you again—why do the gods hate me so? Have pity. You've already killed my brother Polydorus, spare me: among Priam's sons it's Hector you want."

But Achilles looked at him fiercely. "Foolish boy, how can you speak to me of pity? Before you killed Patroclus, I had pity, and spared many Trojans. But now . . . No one will leave my hands alive. Stop whining. A man like Patroclus is dead, who was worth much more than you—why shouldn't you die? Look at me, how strong and handsome I am, and yet I will die. A dawn or sunset or noon will come, and that day will see me die. And you weep for your death?"

Lycaon lowered his head. He reached his arms forward in a final entreaty. Achilles plunged the sword up to the hilt into his body, from top to bottom, entering right under the clavicle. Lycaon crumpled. Achilles took him by the feet and dragged him into my waters. "Your mother will not mourn you on your funeral bed," he said. "But this river will carry you to the sea to be eaten by the fish." Then he started shouting. "You're all going to die! The river won't save you. I'll pursue you to the walls of Troy. You'll die an evil death and pay for what you did to Patroclus." And again he entered the water and began to kill: Asteropaeus, and Thersilochus, and Mydon, and Astypylus, and Mnesus, and Thrasius, and Aenius, and Ophelestes. It was a massacre.

And then I cried, "Get away from me, Achilles, get away if you want to keep killing. Stop piling up corpses in my beautiful waters. I won't have the strength to carry them all to the sea. I am repelled by you, Achilles. Stop or get out."

And Achilles answered me, "I'll go when I've killed them all, River."

Then I stirred up a giant, frightening wave that rose into the air and curled over his shield and plunged down upon him. I saw him looking for something to hold on to. There was an elm on the bank, large and leafy, and he clung to its branches, but the wave carried away the tree, roots and all. It fell headlong into the water, toppling him, too. Then Achilles, with a superhuman effort, stood up and got out of the current and gained the bank, and then he fled toward the plain. And I followed him there. Overflowing my banks, with my waters I followed him, flooding the fields. He fled and the great wave that I had become drove him on; and when he stopped, and turned, I surged over him, and again he found the earth beneath his feet and again began to run, until finally I heard him crying, godlike Achilles, "Mother! Mother! Will no one save me? Why did you tell me I would die beside the walls of Troy? If only Hector, who among them all is the bravest, had killed me. I am a hero, and a hero should kill me. And instead it is fate that I should die a miserable death, overpowered by the river like some poor swineherd!"

He rushed into the water, with corpses and armor floating and swirling all around him. With godlike strength he ran, but I knew that it wouldn't save him, his strength, or his beauty, or his shining armor, that he would end up at the bottom of my swamp, covered with mud, and I would pour cascades of sand and rocks upon him, and forever, forever, I would be his impenetrable tomb. I rose up into the air in a last enormous wave that, churning with foam, and bodies, and blood, would carry him off. Then I saw the fire. From the plain, inexplicable, magic, the fire. A wall of fire moving toward me. The elms, the willows, the tamarisks burned; the lotus and the reeds and the grasses burned; the corpses and the armor and the men burned. I stopped. The fire reached me. What no one had ever seen, everyone saw that day: a river in flames. The water boiling, the fish darting terrified among the glowing pools. So, many nights later, I would see the Trojans flee the burning inferno of their city.

From my bed, having returned, defeated, to my normal currents, I saw Achilles pursue the Trojans to the walls of Ilium. From the height of a tower, Priam observed the defeat. He had the gates thrown open so that his army could take refuge in the city, and he ordered them to be closed again as soon as the last of the soldiers had passed through. But the last was the bravest, the firstborn son, the hero who through that gate would not enter again.

ANDROMACHE

They took refuge in the city like frightened fawns. Priam had had the Scaean gates opened, and they ran inside and ran up on the bastions, still covered with sweat, burning with thirst, and pressed against the parapets to look down onto the plain. Thousands found safety in the belly of the city. Only one remained outside the gates, nailed by his destiny. And it was the man I loved, and the father of my child.

From the distance Achilles arrived, leading his soldiers, swift as a victorious stallion, bright as a star, gleaming like an omen of death. Priam recognized him from the height of the tower and understood. He couldn't restrain himself and began to weep, the old man, the great king, in front of everyone, beating his head with his hands and murmuring, "Hector, my son, flee that place. Achilles is too strong for you, don't face him alone. Can't you see, that man is killing my sons, one by one. Don't you, too, be killed. Save your life and, alive, save the Trojans. I don't want to die run through by a spear the day our city is captured. I don't want to see my sons killed, my daughters taken as slaves, marriage beds devastated, children hurled into the dust in the midst of the massacre. I don't want to end up in the dirt and be torn to pieces by the dogs that, until the day before, I fed with scraps from my table. You, Hector, you're young. The young are beautiful in death, in any death. You mustn't be ashamed to die, but I . . . Think of an old man, and of those dogs standing over him and devouring his head, and tearing his sex from him, and drinking his blood. Think of the white hair, the pale skin. Think of the dogs who then, sated, go and lie down under the portico . . . I am too old, Hector, to die like that. Let me die in peace, my son."

The great king wept. And Hecuba, queen and mother, wept. Her robe was open at the front, and, with her breast bared, she begged her son to remember the time when, a weeping child, he would run to that breast for consolation. Now she wanted him to come to her again, as he had long ago, instead of being killed there, outside the walls, by a cruel man who would have no pity. But Hector wouldn't listen. He stood firm, leaning against the wall, and waited for Achilles, as a snake, swelled with poison, waits for the man in front of his own den. In his heart he mourned the many heroes who had died on that day of war, and knew that he himself had killed them when he refused to pull the army back at the return of Achilles. He had betrayed them, and now the only thing to do was to regain the love of his people by challenging that man. Maybe he thought for an instant of laying down his arms and putting an end to the war, giving back Helen and all her treasures, and others besides. But he knew that nothing now would stop Achilles, except revenge.

He saw him approach, running, radiant in his armor as the rising sun. He saw him stop, the spear raised above his right shoulder, terrible as no man could appear, but only a god. And fear seized his heart. He began to flee, running beside the walls, as fast as he could. Like a falcon, Achilles charged after him, furious. Three times they circled Troy, like horses given their head in a race. But now, in this race, there was no gold, or slaves, or treasure: the prize was Hector's life. And each time they passed the Scaean gates, Achilles went to the inside and cut off Hector's path, pushing him toward the plain, to keep him from escaping into the city. It was like a dream in which we are following someone and can't catch him, but he can't escape, really, either, and it can last all night. It lasted until Deiphobus came out of the Scaean gates and ran swiftly along beside Hector, saying to him, "My brother, Achilles will wear you out. Stop and we'll confront him together."

Hector looked at him and opened his heart to him. "Deiphobus, beloved brother, you alone, seeing me, have had the courage to leave the protection of the walls and come to my aid."

"Our father and mother didn't want me to come," said Deiphobus. "But I couldn't stand it, the anguish was too great, and now I'm here, at your side. Let's stop and fight together: fate will decide if we win, or Achilles."

So that strange dream ended. Hector stopped fleeing. Achilles stopped. Slowly they went toward each other.

The first to speak was Hector. "I won't try to run away from you any longer, Achilles. I've found the courage to face you. Only swear to me that if you win you'll take my armor but not my body. I'll do the same for you."

Achilles looked at him with hatred. "Hector, I curse you. I will not make pacts with you. Men and lions, wolves and lambs don't make pacts: their discord is forever. Think instead about fighting. The moment has arrived to prove that you are really the warrior you think you are."

Then he raised his spear, so that it quivered in the air, and hurled it with terrible force. Hector saw it coming and leaned quickly to one side, so that the bronze tip flew over his shoulder and planted itself in the ground. It was not true, then, that the gods had already decided everything, that the name of the victor was already written! Hector grasped his spear, raised it above his head, and hurled it. The bronze tip hit Achilles' shield in the center, but it was a divine shield; nothing could break it. The bronze point went into the center but stopped there. Hector looked at it in confusion, and turned to ask Deiphobus for another spear so that he could go on fighting. He turned, but Deiphobus was no longer there. He had escaped into the city; fear in the end had borne him away.

Then Hector knew that he had finally met his fate. And since he was a hero, he drew his sword, to die fighting, to die in such a way that all the future generations would tell of it forever. He charged forward, like an eagle greedy for its prey. Facing him, Achilles drew himself up in the splendor of his armor. They leaped on each other like two lions. The bronze tip of Achilles' spear advanced as the evening star advances, shining in the night sky. He looked for an open place in Hector's armor, the armor that had once been his own, and then Patroclus's. He examined the bronze for a crack so that he could get to flesh, and life. He found it at the point where the neck rests on the shoulders, the tender neck of my beloved: the spear pierced the throat and went all the way through.

Hector fell in the dust. He looked at Achilles and with his last breath of life said to him, "I beg you, do not abandon me to the dogs. Give this body to my father."

But the heart of Achilles was hardened against all hope.

"Don't plead with me, Hector. The evil you've done me is too great. It's already something that I won't cut you to pieces and smash you myself. Patroclus will have all the funeral honors that he deserves. You deserve to be eaten by the dogs and the birds, far from your bed, and from the tears of those who loved you."

Hector closed his eyes, and death enveloped him. His soul flew away to Hades, mourning its fate, and lost youth and lost strength.

Achilles pulled his spear from Hector's body. Then he bent down to strip off the armor. All the Achaeans came to watch, close up. For the first time they saw that body naked, without armor. They were amazed by its beauty, and yet not one resisted the temptation to strike him with the sword, with the spear. They laughed. "Hector is certainly a lot softer now than when he was setting fire to our ships." They laughed and they struck him, until Achilles stopped them. He leaned over Hector and with a knife pierced his ankles, just under the anklebone. Through the hole he threaded leather thongs and tied them with strong knots to his chariot. He did it so that the body hung with its head in the dirt. Then he took Hector's armor, his trophy, and mounted the chariot. He whipped the horses and they took off. Hector's body, dragged along the ground, raised a black cloud of dust and blood.

Your face was so beautiful. And now it slides along the ground, with the beautiful hair flying ragged in the dust. We were born in distant places, you in Troy and I in Thebes, but a single fate awaited us. And it was an unhappy fate. Now you leave me a widow in your house, overwhelmed by my tremendous grief. The child we had together is still so young. You can't help him anymore, nor he you. If he should even survive this war, pain and suffering will be his lot forever, because one who has no father loses his friends and struggles to defend his possessions. His gaze lowered, his face lined with tears, he will tug on the cloaks of other fathers for protection, and maybe someone will glance at him with pity, but it will be like wetting the lips of one who is dying of thirst. The Trojans called him "lord of the city," this child, because he was your son, and it was you who, alone, defended the city. Hector . . . Fate caused you to die apart from me, and that will forever be my greatest sorrow, because I didn't have your last words for myself: I would have treasured them and remembered them all my life, every day and every night of my life. Beside the black ships now, you are preyed on by worms, and your naked body, which I so loved, is a meal for the dogs. Fine rich tunics, woven by women's hands, awaited you here. I will go to the palace. I will take them and throw them in the fire. If this is the only pyre I can make in your honor, I will do it. For your glory, before all the men and women of Troy.

PRIAM

And everyone saw the king rolling in the mud, mad with grief. He wandered from one to another, begging them to let him go to the ships of the Achaeans to recover the body of his son. They had to restrain him by force, the mad old man. For days he remained sitting among his sons, wrapped in his cloak, around him only grief and lamentation. Men and women wept, thinking of the lost heroes. The old man waited until the mud hardened on his hair and his pale skin. Then, one evening, he rose. He went to the bedchamber and called his wife, Hecuba. And when she appeared he said, "I must go. I will bring precious gifts that will soften Achilles' heart. I must do it."

Hecuba was in despair. "Gods, where is the wisdom you were famous for? You want to go to the ships, you, by yourself? You want to go to the man who has killed so many of your sons? That man has no pity—do you think he will have pity on you, respect for you? Stay here at home and mourn. For Hector we can do nothing. It was his fate to be devoured by the dogs far away from us, the prey of that man whose liver I would tear out with my teeth."

But the old king answered, "I must go. And you won't stop me. If it is fated that I should die beside the ships of the Achaeans, well, I will die, but not before I hold my son in my arms and shed my tears over him."

Thus he spoke, and he had all the most precious chests opened. He chose twelve of the finest robes, twelve cloaks, twelve blankets, twelve cloths of white linen, and twelve tunics. He weighed ten talents of gold and took two shining tripods, four urns, and a marvelous cup, a gift of the Thracians. Then he hurried out and began shouting furiously at all the people who were lamenting in his house, "Get out, all of you vile people. Don't you have a house of your own where you can go and weep? Do you have to stay here and torment me? Isn't it enough for you that Zeus has taken Hector, who of all my sons was the best, yes, the best? Did you hear me clearly, did you hear me, Paris, and you, Deiphobus, and you, Polites, and Agathon, and Helenus? Worthless, all of you. He was the best. Why didn't you die in his place? Eh? I had brave sons, but I've lost them all, and the worst are left, the vain, the liars, good for dancing and stealing. What are you waiting for, you cowards, go, and get a chariot ready right away. I must go."

They all trembled at the cries of the old king. And you should have seen them, how they ran off to prepare the chariot, and load it with the gifts, and then mules and horses, everything . . . There was no more discussion. When everything was ready, Hecuba came. She held in her right hand a cup of sweet wine. She came to the old king and offered it to him. "If you really want to go," she said, "against my will, at least make an offering to Zeus first, and pray to him to let you return alive."

The old king took the cup, and, since his wife asked him, he raised it to heaven and prayed to Zeus to have pity, and to let him find kindness and compassion where he was going. Then he mounted the chariot. All the gifts had been loaded into a second chariot, driven by Idaeus, the wise herald. The king and his faithful servant departed, without an escort, without warriors, alone, in the dark of the night.

When they reached the river they stopped to let the beasts drink. And there they saw a man approaching, emerging out of nowhere, out of the darkness.

"Let's run away, my king," Idaeus said right away, frightened. "Let's go or he'll kill us."

But I couldn't move. I was petrified with fear. I saw the man getting closer and closer, and I couldn't do a thing. He came toward me, right toward me, and offered me his hand. He looked like a prince, young and handsome.

"Where are you going, old father?" he said. "Don't you fear the fury of the Achaeans, your mortal enemies? If one of them sees you with all that treasure, what will you do? You're no longer young, you two. How will you defend yourselves if someone attacks you? Let me protect you. I won't hurt you: you remind me of my father."

It seemed that a god had put himself in our path. He thought we were escaping from Ilium, that the city was in the grip of terror, and we two had escaped with all the riches we could carry. He knew about the death of Hector and thought the Trojans had fled. And when he spoke of Hector he said: He wasn't inferior to any of the Achaeans in battle.

"Ah, young prince, but who are you, who speak like this of Hector?" And he said that he was a Myrmidon who had come to the war following Achilles and now was one of his attendants. He said that he had seen Hector fight numberless times and remembered when he attacked the ships. And he said that he had come from the camp of the Achaeans, where all the warriors were waiting for dawn to attack Troy again.

"But if you come from there, then you must have seen Hector. Tell me the truth, is he still in Achilles' tent, or have they thrown him out to the dogs?"

"Neither dogs nor birds have devoured him, old man," he answered. "You can't believe it, but his body seems untouched. Twelve days have passed since his death, and yet it's as if he had just died. Every day, at dawn, Achilles pitilessly drags him around the tomb of Patroclus to humiliate him, and every day the body is intact, the wounds close up, the blood disappears. Some god watches over him, old man: even if he is dead, some god loves him."

Ah, I heard those words with joy in my heart . . . I offered him that cup, the cup I had brought for Achilles. I offered it to him and asked him if in exchange he could take us into the Achaean camp.

"Old man, don't test me," he said. "I can't accept gifts from you unbeknownst to Achilles. Anyone who steals something from that man is heading for disaster. But I'll lead you to him without any reward. And you'll see that with me no one will dare stop you." Thus he spoke, and he mounted the chariot, taking the reins and spurring the horses. And when he reached the trench, and the wall, the sentinels said nothing to him. He passed through the open gates and swiftly guided us to Achilles' tent. It was majestic, supported on posts of fir and surrounded by a great courtyard. The enormous door was of wood. The man opened it and told me to enter. "It's as well if Achilles doesn't see me, old man. But don't be afraid, go and kneel before him. May you be able to move his hard heart."

Then the old king entered. He left Idaeus to watch the

chariots. And he entered the tent of Achilles. Some men were busy around the table where they had just been eating. Achilles was sitting in a corner, alone. The old king approached him without anyone noticing. Perhaps he could have killed him. But instead he fell at his feet and embraced his knees. Achilles was startled, caught by surprise. Priam took his hands, the terrible hands that had killed so many of his sons, and brought them to his lips and kissed them. "Achilles, you see me, I am old now. Like your father, I have crossed the threshold of sorrowful old age. But he at least will be in his homeland hoping to see his son return one day from Troy. I, instead, have endured much suffering: fifty sons I had, to defend my land, and the war has taken away almost all of them. Only Hector remained, and you killed him, beside the walls of the city whose last, heroic defender he was. I have come here to bring him home, in exchange for splendid gifts. Have pity on me, Achilles, in memory of your father. If you have pity on him, have pity on me, who, unique among all fathers, was not ashamed to kiss the hand that killed my son."

Achilles' eyes filled with tears. With a gesture he brushed Priam away, but gently. The two men wept, in the memory of a father, a beloved friend, a son. Tears, in the tent, in silence. Then Achilles rose from his chair, took the old king by the hand, and raised him up. He looked at his white hair, his white beard, and, moved, he said, "You unhappy man, who have endured so much heartbreaking sorrow. Where did you find the courage to come to the ships of the Achaeans and kneel before the man who killed so many brave sons? You have a bold spirit, Priam. Sit here, on my chair. Together let's forget our sorrow, which weeping is no help for. It's man's fate to live in sorrow—only the gods live happy. Inscrutable destiny dispenses good and evil. My father, Peleus, was a fortunate man, first among all men, king in his own land, husband of a woman who was a goddess, and yet fate gave him an only son, born to rule, and now that son, far from him, runs swiftly toward his destiny of death, sowing ruin among his enemies. And you, you were so happy once, king of a great land, father of many sons, lord of an immense fortune, and now you are forced every day to wake amid war and death. Be strong, old man, and do not torture yourself: weeping for your son will not bring him back to life." And he gestured the old man to sit on his chair.

But Priam didn't want to. He said he wanted to see the body of his son with his own eyes, that was all he wanted. He didn't want to sit, he wanted his son.

Achilles looked at him in irritation. "Now don't make me angry, old man. I will give you back your son, because if you arrived here alive, it means that it was a god who guided you, and I don't want to displease the gods. But don't make me angry, because I am also capable of disobeying the gods."

The old king then trembled with fear, and sat as he had been ordered. Achilles went out of the tent with his men. He went to get the precious gifts that Priam had chosen for him. And he left two linen cloths and one tunic in the chariot, in which to wrap the body of Hector when it was ready to be carried home. Then he called his servants and ordered them to wash and anoint the body of the hero, and to do all this elsewhere, so that the eyes of Priam wouldn't see and wouldn't suffer. And when the body was ready, Achilles himself took it in his arms, lifted it up, and laid it on the funeral bed. Then he returned to the tent and sat down opposite Priam.

"Your son has been given back to you, old man, as you

wanted. At dawn you will see him, and take him away. And now I order you to eat with me."

They prepared a sort of funeral banquet, and when the meal was over we sat there, facing each other, talking, in the night. I couldn't help admiring his beauty. He was like a god. And he listened to me, in silence, rapt by my words. Incredible as it might seem, we spent the time in admiration of each other, so that at the end, forgetting where I was, and why I was there, I asked for a bed, because it was days since, afflicted by grief, I had slept. And they prepared one for me, with rich carpets and coverings of purple, in a corner, so that none of the other Achaeans should see me. When everything was ready, Achilles came and said to me, "We'll stop the war to give you time to honor your son, old king." And then he took my hand and held it, and I was no longer afraid.

I woke in the middle of the night, when all around me were sleeping. I must have been mad to think of waiting there until dawn. I rose, in silence, and went to the chariots. I woke Idaeus, we hitched the horses, and, without anyone seeing us, we left. We crossed the plain in the darkness. And when golden Aurora slipped over the earth, we arrived at the walls of Troy. From the city the women saw us and began to cry that King Priam had returned, and with him his son Hector, and they streamed out of the gates, running toward us. They all wanted to touch the beautiful head of the dead man, weeping with muted laments. With difficulty the old king managed to drive the chariots inside the walls, and then to the palace. They took Hector and placed him on an inlaid bed. Around him rose the funeral lament. And the women, one by one, went up to him, and holding his head in their hands said farewell.

First was Andromache, who was his wife. "Hector, by dying young you leave me a widow in our house, with a small child who will never grow up. This city will be destroyed, because you who protected it are dead. The wives of the princes will be dragged onto the ships, and I will be among them. One of the Achaeans will take your son and hurl him down from the high towers, giving him a horrible death, in hatred and contempt for you who killed so many sons of the Achaeans, and brothers, and friends. Your parents mourn you today, the whole city mourns you, but no one mourns you with such sorrow as your wife, who will never forget that you died far away from her."

Then Hecuba grieved for him: the mother. "Hector, among all my sons the dearest to my heart. The gods who loved you so much in life even in death have not abandoned you. Achilles dragged you on the ground, to make his beloved friend Patroclus happy, but now I find you here and you are beautiful, and fresh, and whole. Achilles destroyed you with his spear, but I think you died a sweet death, my son."

And finally Helen of Argos mourned him. "Hector, my friend. Twenty years have passed since Paris took me away from my homeland. And in twenty years never once did I hear from you an unkind word or an insult. And if someone spoke ill of me, here in the palace, you always defended me with sweet, gentle words. I weep for you because in you I mourn the only friend I had. You're gone, leaving me alone to be devoured by hatred."

So they mourned through the night, the women and men of Troy, around the body of Hector, breaker of horses. The next day, they built a pyre in his honor and let the flames flare up high in the rosy light of dawn. They stored his white bones in a golden urn, wrapped in a purple cloth. The bones repose now in the depths of the earth, where no Achaean warrior can ever disturb them.

DEMODOCUS

Many years after these events, I was at the court of the Phaeacians when a mysterious man arrived from the sea, who had been shipwrecked and had no name. He was welcomed like a king, and honored with all the rites of hospitality. During the sumptuous banquet prepared for him, I sang the adventures of heroes, because I am a bard and singing is my work. The man listened, sitting in the place of honor. He listened to me in silence, filled with emotion. And when I finished he cut a piece of meat and offered it to me, and said, "Demodocus, a Muse, a daughter of Zeus, was your master, for you sing the stories of the Achaean heroes with wonderful art. I would like to hear in your voice the story of the wooden horse, the trap that godlike Odysseus devised for the destruction of Ilium. Sing it, and I will tell everyone that a god taught you to sing." This he asked me, the man without a name. And this is what I sang for him, and for all.

. . .

Already the tenth year had passed and the war was still going on between Achaeans and Trojans. The spears were tired of killing, the straps of the shields, worn out, were breaking, and the weakened bowstrings let the swift arrows fall. The horses, grown old, grazed sadly, heads lowered, eyes closed, mourning the companions with whom they had run and fought. Achilles lay under the earth beside his beloved Patroclus. Nestor wept for his son Antilochus; Telamonian Ajax wandered through Hades after killing himself; Paris, the cause of the evil, was dead, and Helen lived with her new husband, Deiphobus, son of Priam. The Trojans mourned Hector, and Sarpedon, and Rhesus. Ten years. And Troy still rose intact in the shelter of its invincible walls.

It was Odysseus who invented the end of that endless war. He ordered Epeus to construct a giant wooden horse. Epeus was the best when it came to making instruments or machines for war. He set to the work. He had tree trunks brought down from the mountains, the same wood with which many years before the Trojans had built the ships of Paris, the origin of the evil. Epeus used the wood to build the horse. He began with the belly, broad and hollow. Then he attached the neck, and on the purple mane he poured pure gold. In place of the eyes he put precious stones: the green emerald and the blood-colored amethyst sparkled together. To the temples he attached the ears, pricked as if to grasp in the silence the sound of the war trumpet. Then he put on the back, the sides, and finally the legs, bending them at the knees, as if they were running, a motionless but true gait. The hooves were of bronze, plated with gleaming tortoiseshell. In the side of the animal the genius of Epeus cut a small, invisible door, and attached a ladder that when needed could let men go up and down, and then disappear inside the horse. He worked for days. But finally the marvelous horse appeared: gigantic, to the eyes of the Achaeans, and terrifying.

Then Odysseus called the princes to an assembly. And, in that deep voice that was his alone, he spoke. "Friends, you continue to have faith in your weapons, and in your courage. But meanwhile we're growing old here, without glory, exhausting ourselves in a war without end. Believe me, only by intelligence, not by force, will we take Troy. Do you see that, the magnificent wooden horse built by Epeus? Listen to my plan: Some of us will climb inside it, fearlessly. The others, after burning the encampment, will set sail for the open sea, leaving the beach deserted, and will go and hide behind the island of Tenedos. The Trojans will have to believe that we've really gone. They'll see the horse: they'll take it for a homage to their valor, or a gift to the goddess Athena. Trust me: they will bring it into their city, and it will be their end."

Thus he spoke. And they listened. And they had faith in him. They drew lots to see who would go inside the horse. And the lots indicated five of them: Odysseus, Menelaus, Diomedes, Anticlus, and Neoptolemus, who was the son of Achilles. They climbed inside the horse, and then they closed the little door that Epeus had cut in the wood. They crouched down in the darkness with anguish in their hearts. They were like animals who, frightened by a storm, have taken refuge in their den and now await the sun's return, tormented by hunger and unease.

The others meanwhile waited for night, and when it was dark they destroyed their encampments and put the ships to sea. Before dawn rose they had gained the open sea and disappeared behind the island of Tenedos. On the beach, where the immense army had lived for ten years, there remained only corpses and smoking ruins.

Amid the first shadows of breaking day, the Trojans saw, far off, the smoke of the fires. The news that the Achaeans had fled spread quickly, echoing again and again from one to another, a cry of ever-increasing hope and joy. They emerged from behind the walls, just a few at a time, and then in greater numbers, and crossed the plain to see. When Priam arrived, surrounded by the old men of Troy, what he saw was an immense empty beach, in the middle of which towered a gigantic wooden horse. They gathered around that marvel. Some, because of their hatred for the Achaeans, wanted to throw it into the sea or hack it to pieces with axes; but others, seduced by the beauty of the horse, urged that it be consecrated to the gods and brought into the city as a magnificent monument to the war that had been won. And in the end they prevailed, because men are pitiful, and it is not given to them to see the future, but only to live enveloped in the fog of the present. They drove the horse on its speeding wheels over the plain, accompanying it with singing and dancing. Loud were the cries of the men who were pulling the thick ropes, who by their great effort were dragging into their dwelling place an animal with poisonous entrails. When they arrived at the wall, they had to widen the gates to get the giant horse into the city. But this, too, they did amid dancing and singing, while they scattered a carpet of flowers where the animal would pass and sprinkled honey and perfumes everywhere.

Then Cassandra, the daughter of Priam, appeared, who had received from the gods the gift of being able to read the future and the punishment of never being believed. She appeared like a fury in the middle of that celebration, tearing her hair and her clothes and crying. "Wretched people, what is this horse of misfortune that you are driving like madmen? You are rushing toward your darkest night. This creature is pregnant with enemy soldiers, and it will give birth to them in the night under the affectionate gaze of Athena, the destroyer of cities. And an ocean of blood will run in these streets, overwhelming us all in a great wave of death. Ah, beloved city of my ancestors, you will soon be ashes in the wind. Father, Mother, I beg you, return to yourselves and send away this horror. Destroy that horse, burn it, and then indeed we will celebrate with singing and dancing. Only then will we rejoice at freedom regained, freedom that we so love."

Cassandra cried out. But no one would listen to her. And her father, Priam, reproached her violently. "Prophetess of doom, what evil divinity has possessed you this time? Does our joy distress you? Can't you let us celebrate in peace this long-awaited day of freedom? The war is over, Cassandra. And this horse isn't doom but a worthy gift for Athena, the patron goddess of our city. Go, return to the palace, we no longer need you. From today onward, there is to be no more fear in the shadow of the walls of Troy, but only joy, and celebration, and liberty." So Cassandra was dragged into the darkness of the palace by force. In her eyes Troy was already burning in the leaping flames of ruin.

They brought the horse to the temple of Athena, placing it on a high pedestal. All around, the people indulged in the most unrestrained joy, abandoning themselves to their folly and forgetting all caution. A few sentries stood at the gates, survivors of a war that was thought to be over. Finally, in the rosy light of sunset, Helen of Argos came out of the palace, brilliantly arrayed. Under the admiring eyes of the Trojans she crossed the city and arrived at the feet of the giant horse. Then she did a strange thing. She circled around it three times, imitating the

voices of the wives of the Achaean heroes hidden inside, calling them, and begging them to come to her arms. Enclosed in
the blind darkness of the belly of the horse, the five Achaeans
felt their hearts breaking. It really was the voices of their
wives, however incredible; it was their voices, and the voices
were calling them. It was a cruel sweetness, and they all felt
the tears rise in their eyes, and anguish swelled their hearts.
Suddenly Anticlus, who was the weakest and the most inexpe-
rienced, opened his mouth to cry out. Odysseus jumped on
him and pressed his hands over his mouth, both hands, force-
fully. Anticlus began to wriggle, trying desperately to free himself. But implacable Odysseus pressed his hands over his
mouth and didn't stop until Anticlus gave a shudder and then
another, and a last, violent jolt, and then died, suffocated.

At the feet of the horse, Helen of Argos threw a last glance
at the mute belly of the creature. Then she turned and went
back to the palace.

The whole city, then, sank into slumber. Flutes and pipes
slid from hands, and the last barking of the dogs punctuated
the silence that is the companion of peace.

In the still night, a torch shone, to give the sign to the
Achaean fleet. A traitor let it shine high in the darkness. But
some say that it was Helen of Argos herself who betrayed
Troy. And while the Achaean ships returned to the beach, and
in silence the army flooded the plain, from the belly of the
horse came Odysseus, Menelaus, Diomedes, and Neoptolemus. Like lions they set on the sentries at the gates, shedding
the first blood of that terrible night. The first shouts rose into
the sky over Troy. Mothers woke without understanding, hugging their children and grieving softly, like swallows. Men
turned in their sleep with presentiments of doom, dreaming of
their own death. When the Achaean army came through the

gates, the massacre began. Widow of her warriors, the city began to vomit corpses. Men died without time to seize their weapons, women died without even trying to escape. The children died in their arms and, in their wombs, the unborn. Old men died without dignity as, lying on the ground, they raised their arms begging to be spared. Dogs and birds, intoxicated, went wild fighting for the blood and flesh of the dead.

In the midst of the massacre Odysseus and Menelaus rushed about, looking for the rooms of Helen and Deiphobus: they wanted to take back what they had so long been fighting for. They surprised Deiphobus as he tried to escape. Menelaus thrust the sword into his stomach. His guts poured out on the ground and Deiphobus fell, oblivious of war and chariots forever. They found Helen in her rooms. She followed her old husband, trembling. In her heart she felt relief for the end of her misfortune, and shame for what it had been.

Now I should sing of that night. I should sing of Priam, killed at the foot of the altar of Zeus, and little Astyanax, hurled by Odysseus down from the walls, and the lament of Andromache, and the shame of Hecuba, dragged off like a slave, and the terror of Cassandra, raped by Oilean Ajax on the altar of Athena. I should sing of a race that was butchered, and a beautiful city that became a flaming pyre and the silent tomb of its sons. I should sing of that night, but I am only a bard. Let the Muses do it, if they can. A night of such sorrow I will not sing.

Thus I spoke. Then I realized that that man, the man without a name, was weeping. He wept like a woman, like a wife bent over the man she loves who has been murdered by his enemies. He wept like a girl captured by a soldier, a slave forever. Alcinous, the king, realized it, sitting next to him, and nodded to me to stop singing. Then he leaned toward the stranger and said, "Why do you weep, friend, hearing the story of Ilium? It was the gods who willed that night of blood, and those men died so that afterward they would be sung of forever. Why does their story make you suffer? Maybe on that night your father, your brother died, or you lost a friend in that war? Do not be obstinate in your silence, and tell me who you are and where you are from, and who is your father. No one comes into the world without a name, however rich or poor. Tell me your name, stranger."

The man lowered his gaze. Then he said softly, "I am Odysseus. I come from Ithaca and there, one day, I will return."

ANOTHER KIND OF BEAUTY: NOTE ON WAR

This is not just an ordinary time in which to read the *Iliad*. Or, rather, to rewrite it, as I have done. This is a time of war. And although "war" seems to me the wrong word to describe what is happening in the world (a term of convenience, I would call it), certainly it is a time when a kind of prideful barbarism that for millennia was linked to the experience of war has again become a daily experience. Battles, assassinations, bombings, torture, decapitations, betrayals. Heroism, weapons, strategic plans, volunteers, ultimatums, proclamations. From some depths that we thought were sealed, the whole atrocious and shining armamentarium that from time immemorial has been the escort of mankind at war has returned to the surface. In such a context—extremely delicate and shocking—even the details take on a particular significance. To read the *Iliad* in public is a detail, but it is not an ordinary detail. To be clear, I would like to say that the *Iliad* is a story of war, without caution and without half measures, and that it was composed in order to sing of mankind at war, and to do it in a way so memorable that it would endure into eternity, as far as the last child of a child, continuing to sing of the solemn beauty, and the immutable emotion, that war once was and always will be. In school, maybe, they tell it differently. But the point is this. The *Iliad* is a monument to war.

So the question naturally arises: what meaning does it have at a time like this to dedicate so much space and attention and time to a monument to war? How in the world, when there are so many stories, does one find oneself drawn to that one, as if it were a light that dictated a flight into the darkness of these days?

I think a true answer could be given only if one were capable of understanding completely our relationship to *all* stories of war, and not this one in particular: understanding our instinct to never stop telling those stories. But it's a complex matter, which certainly can't be resolved here, and by me. What I can do is stay with the *Iliad* and note two things that, in a year of working closely with the text, occurred to me: two things that summarize what in that story appeared to me with the force and clarity that only true lessons have.

The first. One of the surprising things in the *Iliad* is the power, I would even say compassion, with which the motivations of the conquered are conveyed. It's a story written by the conquerors, and yet our memory preserves also, if not above all, the human figures of the Trojans: Priam, Hector, Andromache, even minor characters like Pandarus and Sarpedon. I found, working on the text, this supernatural capacity to be the voice of all humanity and not only of themselves, and discovered how the Greeks have handed down, in the *Iliad*, between the lines of a monument to war, the memory of a stubborn love for peace. At first sight, blinded by the brightness of

armor and heroes, you don't realize it. But in the shadow of
reflection an *Iliad* that you don't expect emerges. I mean the
feminine side of the *Iliad*. It's often the women who express,
without mediation, the desire for peace. Relegated to the margins of combat, they embody the persistent and almost clan-
destine hypothesis of an alternative civilization, free from the
duty of war. They are convinced that one could live in a different way, and they say so. They say it most clearly in Book 6, a
small masterpiece of sentimental geometry. In a suspended
moment, empty, stolen from battle, Hector enters the city and
meets three women, and it's like a journey to the other side of
the world. On close examination, all three utter the same
plea—for peace—but each with her own emotional tonality.
His mother asks him to pray. Helen invites him to sit beside her
and rest (and also something more, perhaps). Andromache,
finally, asks him to be father and husband ahead of hero and
fighter. Especially in this last dialogue, the synthesis is of an
almost didactic clarity: two possible worlds stand facing each
other, and each has its arguments. Tougher, blinder, those of
Hector; modern, much more human, those of Andromache. Is
it not remarkable that a male and warlike civilization like that
of the Greeks chose to hand down, into eternity, the voice of
women and their desire for peace?

One learns about the feminine side of the *Iliad* from that
voice, but, once you've learned about it, you find it everywhere, shadowy, almost imperceptible, but incredibly tenacious. I see it very strongly in the innumerable places in the
Iliad in which the heroes, instead of fighting, talk. There are
assemblies that never end, interminable debates, and you stop
hating them only when you begin to understand what in fact
they are: a way of putting off the battle as long as possible.
They are Scheherazade, who saves herself by telling stories.

The word is the weapon with which men freeze the war. Even when they are discussing how to carry on the war, they're not carrying it on, and this is always a way of saving themselves. They are all condemned to death, but they make the final cigarette last an eternity, and they smoke it with the words. Then, when they do go into battle, they are transformed into blind heroes, forgetful of escape, fanatically devoted to duty. But first: first is a long time, feminine, a time of knowing delays and childish backward looks.

This sort of reluctance of the hero is, rightly, concentrated to the highest and most dazzling degree in Achilles. It is he who takes the longest time, in the *Iliad,* to go into battle. It is he who, like a woman, is present at the war from a distance, playing a lyre and staying beside those he loves. The very one who is the most ferocious and fanatical, a literally superhuman incarnation of war. The geometry of the *Iliad* is, in this, of a stunning precision. Where the triumph of warrior culture is strongest, the more tenacious and persistent is the feminine inclination to peace. Finally, what can't be confessed by the heroes erupts in Achilles, in the unmediated clarity of explicit and definitive speech. What he says to the delegation sent by Agamemnon, in Book 9, is perhaps the most violent and incontrovertible cry for peace that our fathers have handed down to us:

Nothing, for me, is worth life: not the treasures that the prosperous city of Ilium possessed before, in time of peace, before the sons of the Danaans arrived; not the riches that, beyond the stone threshold, the temple of Apollo, lord of arrows, in rocky Pythos, contains; oxen and fat sheep can be stolen, tripods and tawny-maned horses can be bought; but the life of a man does not come back, one cannot steal or buy it, once it has passed the barrier of the teeth.

They are words for Andromache, but in the *Iliad* Achilles
utters them, the high priest of the religion of war, and so they
resound with an unmatched authority. In that voice—which,
buried under a monument to war, says farewell to war, choos-
ing life—the *Iliad* lets us glimpse a civilization that the Greeks
could not achieve and yet had an intuition of, and knew, and
even preserved in a secret and protected corner of their feel-
ings. Bringing to fulfillment that intuition is perhaps what the
Iliad offers as our inheritance, and task, and duty.

How to undertake such a task? What must we do to induce
the world to follow its own inclination for peace? About this,
too, it seems to me, the *Iliad* has something to teach us. And it
does so in its most obvious and shocking aspect: its warrior
and masculine aspect. It's indisputable that the story presents
war as an almost natural outlet of civil life. But it doesn't con-
fine itself to that. It does something much more important
and, if you like, intolerable: it sings the *beauty* of war, and
does so with memorable power and passion. There is almost
no hero whose splendor, moral and physical, at the moment of
combat we do not recall. There is almost no death that is not
an altar, richly decorated and adorned with poetry. The fasci-
nation with arms and armor is invariable, and admiration for
the aesthetic beauty of the movement of armies is constant.
The animals in war are beautiful, and nature is solemn when it
is called on to frame the slaughter. Even the blows and wounds
are celebrated as lofty creations of a paradoxically cruel but
accomplished artisan. One would say that everything, from
the men to the earth, finds in the experience of war its highest
realization, both aesthetic and moral: like the glorious peak of
a parabola that only in the atrocity of a mortal clash finds its
fulfillment. In this homage to the beauty of war the *Iliad* forces

us to recall something disturbing but inexorably true: for millennia war has been for men the circumstance in which the intensity—the beauty—of life is released in all its power and truth. It was almost the only possibility for changing one's destiny, for discovering the truth of oneself, for gaining a high ethical knowledge. In contrast to the anemic emotions of life and the mediocre moral stature of the everyday, war sets the world in motion and thrusts individuals outside their accustomed confines into a place of the soul that must seem to them, at last, the harbor of every seeking and every desire. I am not speaking of distant, primitive times: just a few years ago, refined intellectuals like Wittgenstein and Gadda obstinately sought the front line, the front, in an inhuman war, with the conviction that only there would they find themselves. They were not weak individuals, or without means and culture. And yet, as their diaries testify, they lived in the conviction that that peak experience—the atrocious practice of mortal combat—could offer them what daily life was unable to express. This conviction reflects the profile of a civilization that never died and in which war remained the burning fulcrum of human experience, the engine of any becoming. Even today, in a time when for the majority of human beings the hypothesis of going into battle is little more than an absurdity, we continue to feed, with wars fought by proxy with the bodies of professional soldiers, the old brazier of the warrior spirit, betraying our serious incapacity to find a meaning in life that can forgo that moment of truth. The ill-concealed masculine pride that, in the West as in the Islamic world, has accompanied the latest warrior exhibitions lets us recognize an instinct that the shock of the wars of the twentieth century has evidently not put to sleep. The *Iliad* describes this system of thought and this mode of feeling, concentrating it under a synthetic and perfect sign: beauty. The beauty of war—of each of its details—expresses its centrality in human experience, conveys the idea that there is nothing else, in human experience, that enables one to truly exist.

What the *Iliad* perhaps suggests is that pacifism, today, must not forget or deny that beauty, as if it had never existed. To say and teach that war is hell and that's all is a damaging lie. Although it sounds terrible, we must remember that war is hell—*but beautiful*. Men have always thrown themselves into it, drawn like moths to the fatal light of the flame. There is no fear, or horror of themselves, that has succeeded in keeping them from the flame, because in it they find the only possible recompense for the shadows of life. For this reason, today, the task of a true pacifism should be not to demonize war excessively so much as to understand that only when we are capable of another kind of beauty will we be able to do without what war has always offered us. To construct another kind of beauty is perhaps the only route to true peace. To show ourselves capable of illuminating the shadows of existence without recourse to the flame of war. To give a powerful meaning to things without having to place them in the blinding light of death. To be able to change one's own destiny without having to take possession of another's; to mobilize money and wealth without having recourse to violence; to find an ethical dimension, the highest, without having to search for it at the margins of death; to find oneself in the intensity of places and moments that are not a trench; to know emotion, even the most impassioned, without having to resort to the drug of war or the methadone of small daily acts of violence. Another kind of beauty, if you know what I mean.

Today peace is little more than a political convenience. It's certainly not a truly widespread system of thought and way of feeling. War is considered an evil to avoid, of course, but it is far from being considered an absolute evil. At the first occasion, clothed in beautiful ideas, going into battle quickly becomes a real option again. At times it is even chosen with a certain pride. The moths continue to destruct in the light of the flame. A real, prophetic, and courageous ambition for peace I see only in the patient and secret work of millions of artists who every day work to create *another kind of beauty,* and the glow of bright lights that do not kill. It's a utopian undertaking, which assumes an extreme trust in man. But I wonder if we have ever gone so far on such a path as we have today. And for that reason I think that no one, now, will any longer be able to stop that movement, or change its direction. We will succeed, sooner or later, in taking Achilles away from that fatal war. And it will not be fear or horror that carries him home. It will be a different sort of beauty, more dazzling than his, and infinitely more gentle.